Bitter Oranges

Bitter Oranges

Basma Elkhatib

Translated by:
Paula Haydar

Hamad bin Khalifa University Press
P O Box 5825
Doha, Qatar

www.hbkupress.com

All rights reserved.

No part of this publication may be reproduced or transmitted in any form or by any means, electronic or mechanical, including photocopying, recording, or any information storage or retrieval system, without prior permission in writing from the publishers.

No responsibility for loss caused to any individual or organization acting on or refraining from action as a result of the material in this publication can be accepted by HBKU Press or the author.

First English edition in 2022

ISBN: 9789927161124

Printed in Beirut-Lebanon

Qatar National Library Cataloging-in-Publication (CIP)

Elkhatib, Basma, author.

[برتقال مر]. English

Bitter oranges / by Basma Elkhatib ; Translated by Paula Haydar. First English edition. – Doha, Qatar : Hamad Bin Khalifa University Press, 2022.

pages ; cm

ISBN 978-992-716-112-4
Translation of: برتقال مر.

1. Arabic fiction -- Translations into English. 2. Novels. I. Haydar, Paula, translator. II. Title.

PZ10.731 .K4313 2022
892.737 – dc 23   202228432666

Dedication:
> For my grandmother, Najiya: your name predicted are fate,
> for we our both survivors.

Part One

1

The darkness is not pitch-black—more like a grey curtain.

I can see their ghosts—the women who started gathering up my bones from between the cracks in the ground with chapped, chubby fingers—the same fingers with which they gather up olives, picking them out from between the thorns and pebbles.

I heard my bones breaking into pieces over the dry, crumbling dirt as my grandmother screamed in terror, "The little girl is dead. She's dead!"

And then, of course, came music.

That music I don't know how to describe. I hum it in my most desperate moments, aware of how it will always keep me company from behind the wall I lean on, but don't see—will never see. Because, most likely, it is music I don't really hear but only imagine floating around me—surrounding me like a halo—aiming its sad tunes at my back which shudders and heaves against my chest in fear of it, waking me from my nightmare.

I wake up but don't open my eyes, preferring to contemplate the inky blackness of my closed eyelids.

I like imagining the darkness is still there, and I haven't opened my eyes at all. Perhaps what happened next is merely a nightmare unfolding in the darkness of a young girl's grave on whose headstone is etched 1970–1975?

The story could have ended early—without regret— and I allowed to die, light and innocent. If only the ground hadn't been saturated with the rains of the day before, and the one heading towards me had been Aisha, as I had thought, and not my grandmother. Things might've been different had she not come outside to snatch me from the jaws of death as she brushed off the mud with her skirt, letting the air enter through my nose. Had our neighbor not sought the only medical student in the quarter to treat me and stitch up the tear in my neck, the smell of anesthesia on his fingers, the lingering scent of his cologne would not have settled between the stitches, where they remain to this day.

Few know there is a scar on my neck. I must lift my head and cup my hair up for it to show clearly. When

I leave the house, I make sure to conceal it, not only out of embarrassment, but from the weariness of having to recall its provenance.

Only the women in the quarter and some relatives know about it. That is due to my careful habit of keeping my hair beneath the embroidered scarf I wear around the house. It's not only for the sake of cleanliness, but also out of an aversion to seeing hair flowing loosely while inside the house—especially in the kitchen. It's also for my dislike at the tingling sensation of hair on my face and neck. Because of it, I'm always tilting my head and tucking my hair under the scarf. That's when people might see my scar, which looks like the distant trail left in the sand by a snake.

"What's it from? A fall? A sickle?" I am often asked.

I used to go on at length. Then the details became too painful, and a reminder of what I didn't say hurt me more—hiding my yearning for the one who had stitched the scar and touched something much deeper than a surface wound.

Later, I explained it away with casual brevity—a childish insouciance—as if the story was really very simple, "I was holding a bird at the edge of the balcony. The bird flew off, so I went after it, and I fell. That's all there is to it."

In a way, that is exactly what happened. When I was so little, the angels took pity on me and planted two wings on my back.

I was holding the bird in one hand and, with the other, I was trying to tie its leg to a string.

Sensing Aisha's footsteps approaching, I clung to the edge of the crumbling balcony.

"She's going to take him away from me!" I cried. "She's going to strangle him!"

I tried to tie him quickly, but the footsteps came ever closer. As the tiny bird trembled in my hands, my own heart fluttered. Heaven knows which of us was more frightened, weaker, or had a greater desire to flee.

Aisha is following me. She's going to strangle him just as she has done to all my birds—the ones my father brings home alive, and which I find dead the next morning.

He squawked and shook his feathers in my face. It hurt, so I let him go.

For a moment, I resisted the urge to go after him. The string was still in my hand, but then I wasn't on the edge of the balcony anymore.

As if a bird myself, I began to hover in the air. For how long I couldn't say because I was preoccupied with searching for my bird.

As I floated in the air, the scent of the distant sea wafted by. It was mixed with smells from the muddy brook, some chicken manure, and cinnamon emanating from a nearby kitchen.

The air blew into my linen dress, filling it up like a balloon. Then its heaviness filled my chest, nose and mouth, and I had somehow forgotten to breathe.

When I hit the ground, I searched the sky for my little bird, but he'd seen his chance of escape and taken it.

Soon, the sky and clouds became obscured by the face of my grandmother who was peering over the metal railing of the balcony. She called down to me, her face full of horror. My name flashed and disappeared—two consonants, a number equivalent to zero in the world of names—as if I am nameless, and it wouldn't make any difference if I died.

"The little girl is dead…dead!" she cried.

I had no conception of death, only of the ghouls and wolves that died in grandmother's stories. Later on, she would not tell the stories about my miscarried uncles—and that's why I wasn't afraid as I fell, and my grandmother wailed.

Even after the rusty balcony railing was taken down and a more secure one was built, when she had become acquainted with the term "veranda" instead of "tercina"—an old type of balcony—I remained standing in the same spot, trying to measure the distance and time of the fall.

I toss a bitter orange or a marble and count the time it takes to reach the ground. It is very short—just a few seconds. But I drag out the counting because the moment of my fall lasted a long time. During that time, songs played in my eardrums that were packed with tears, strange odors wafted by, and I glimpsed many faces—interspersed between them the faces of my grandmother and of the young medical student who treated me.

"What's your name?" he asked.

I remained mute—caught in the shock of the moment.

"How old are you?" he continued.

"I…"

"Okay. How many do you see?"

He moved something towards my eyes—his fingers perhaps—but I couldn't make it out. My senses were out of sync. Only the strongest one still worked—my sense of smell.

I didn't answer his questions. Nothing stayed with me but my bird.

I tried to scream but was unable. The urge to cry came, but I couldn't feel my eyes. Perhaps I was still falling—in that space between the balcony and the brook, and I was now on my way to the valley and the brook that had dug out its belly. Maybe the soil wouldn't be soft this time, and the rain will have abandoned it a distant winter ago.

***

Beads of sweat trickle behind my left ear and form a pool along the rippled scar line.

A painful midday? In vain, I try to sleep. Time in this city is longer than in my village.

I am supposed to get some sleep. That was what Suha the manicurist advised so my skin could rest up for the party.

I didn't tell her it wasn't a party. I was afraid of being exposed if I said anything. Ridicule of my accent taught me to be silent, not calm, the proof being that Suha kept telling me to relax between one minute and the next. I was embarrassed to tell her that it was the first time I ever had my nails manicured at a beauty salon, where I had allowed a man to massage my feet, file the dead skin off them and pass his fingers between my toes!

"Please relax…relax," she pleaded, while I was left wondering how I could possibly loosen up.

I could apologize for the appearance of my fingers that were not accustomed to being pampered or taken care of. I could tell her that since childhood I have been overworking them in the kitchen and in the fields. But I was also ashamed to make excuses. Then I thought about apologizing for being ashamed…it was a never-ending cycle, and it gave me the usual midday headache.

I walk around the kitchen, allowing such thoughts to disturb my equilibrium.

I take a third sedative.

The refrigerator is about to burst. I make room for the soaked chickpeas beside the chicken marinating in rosemary, garlic, and wild thyme. One cannot take a chance leaving anything out where the temperature is above 35 degrees Celsius. The vegetables, the meat and everything I prepared are all stuffed into the refrigerator.

The banquet must be a success. If I overlook any detail, I'll be ruined.

I touch the scar.

It's still there. It didn't get buried by the sand dunes of insomnia.

I feel it has swelled up from the heat and excitement.

It excites me that I moved to Beirut to be closer to you, and that you don't know that I am here or what my plan is, and that I will meet you after long years of waiting for this encounter. Longing and fear tear at my heart, so my fatigue doubles and the scar throbs with twice the pain.

I slip into the shower for the second time. The water from the roof flows hot yet no longer produces the desired effect. I turn the faucet off and sit there in the cracked tub. The last drops of water make their exit down the drain. They fall into the darkness the same way I fall whenever I go to sleep troubled. I let my hair dry, the evaporating water cooling my back. I finger the strands and ask myself how it will look tomorrow after I come back from the hairdresser.

Heavy are the wet strands. Heavy with memories and fear.

***

I was five. I wasn't going to school because no one paid attention to my age. I didn't have to comb my hair in the morning, but at a certain time during the day, she would call me and sit me down to comb my hair, her head towering over me.

I buried that comb in the ground—the one she dipped in water before sinking it into my hair. I buried lots of combs, so she put me over those hard knees of hers that were like two slabs of granite, grabbed hold of the copious tangled strands and started cutting them right at the scalp. The cold metal of the scissors cut through my hair like a snow plough.

"It's not enough that you're always feverish! Sickly child! You had to have thick, coarse hair to drive me crazy, too? Everything about you annoys me! But that's it. Now you'll see. I'll be free of your nastiness for good. Show me where you're going to bury the comb now!"

My screaming brought the neighbors over—my uncle's wife Nabiha at the front of the pack.

Mouths agape, shock appeared on their faces. A little girl with a prisoner's haircut and the face of a criminal, gasping for the nearest rescuer.

Besides the scar on my neck, the scars on my head also showed—the ones from the mischief of my five years of childhood. And my eyebrows looked thicker. My aunt took me to the nearest barber, to rescue what she could. The women of the village didn't have women's hair salons at that time.

The barber ridiculed us both, but he saved his curses for Aisha. He sat me down in front of a rusty mirror. I closed my eyes to shut out the frightening creature I'd become. But the spots of rust that studded my eyelid appeared through the cracks.

When my sisters returned from school and saw me, they broke into uncontrollable giggles. My sister Zalfa brought me a scarf and wrapped it around my head to avoid seeing that repulsive sight. Inadvertently, she had also helped ease my own fear by protecting me from the harmful winter cold.

Then the smell of fresh bird blood wafted past my nose, and I caught sight of their shivering feathers. My father was home for lunch.

Dangling from his waist were the birds he killed twice—once with the buckshot and once by cutting their throats—something I could never appreciate. He put the quail shot rifle down on the patched-up sofa.

My sisters rushed to prepare his lunch while he washed the bird blood and feathers off his hands. He ate in silence without commenting on my condition. When he'd eaten his fill and burped, he pulled out a lottery ticket from the place where he hid those tickets he got from Beirut. Before leaving, he asked me with a calm exterior, "What did you do to yourself?"

"Mother cut her hair because she had lice," Saada answered.

"No, not because of lice," Manal corrected. "She cut it because it was a knotted mess."

"Well, okay! She wished so hard for a boy, God finally sent her one, but without the right body parts!" he said, without emotion, and then took off with the lottery ticket and his birds.

The term "*Sahbeh*—Lottery" was never far from him. It was his trade, his nickname, and the story of his life…and his death, too.

He would enter the "coffee house" or sit at the door, and men would approach or call to him. They'd give him a little bit of money in return for one of the possible names written on the "lottery ticket." Once all the names were bought, it was time for the draw. He would tear the stub off the ticket to see which name was on it, and that person would win the birds.

It was not an insignificant prize. Birds were a delicacy that most of the coffee house regulars devoured with delight, as did the transient customers and strangers who sought us out to buy olive oil, soap, or orange blossom water…

He never tried to rid himself of the "*Sahbeh*," label because he knew the nickname would stick to him forever. He had inherited it from his father, and I inherited it from both of them.

Everywhere, everyone introduced me as "*Bint Sahbeh*—Sahbeh's daughter". And Aisha was called "Sahbeh's wife," and my five sisters were "Sahbeh's little girls."

I am Bint Sahbeh in name and in likeness. They know it from my face and from my thick eyebrows. And with that haircut, I became his son, not just his daughter.

When my grandmother saw me with that horrifying appearance, she felt sorry for me. She backed away from the hot laundry cauldron and with her blackened fingers—from the burnt firewood—she pulled out her little worn-out and peeling purse from her bosom and gave me a quarter lira coin.

That was the biggest opportunity in my five years of life.

I was not enticed by candy, chocolates or salted nuts. My dreams lay elsewhere.

The bookstore.

I held the quarter up in clear view as I entered the bookstore, so he wouldn't kick me out the front door as he usually did.

Every day, I would stop in front of the bookstore and peer through the window at the colored pencils and exciting storybooks—the stories of Little Red Riding Hood, Cinderella and Sleeping Beauty—and he would yell at me and shoo me away for standing there too long, blocking the view of potential customers.

Unable to read, I didn't care much for the titles, but the covers were guaranteed to enchant me—drawings of pretty girls in captivating dresses with long, wide petticoats, their soft blond hair so long, it flowed down their slender back. There was always a handsome prince too, and the palaces and the green meadows. My dream was to buy those storybooks, or one of them at least.

I chose one with a picture on its cover of a blonde girl in a beautiful pearly dress. Standing over her head was a fairy with a magic wand showering her with flowers and stars!

I held up the quarter lira and asked about the price of the book, but that didn't do me any good.

Without a word, he came over and slapped me, and the quarter fell from my hand. The bookstore turned dark and gloomy, and so did the princess's face. Her shiny dress was snuffed out. I couldn't locate the quarter anywhere despite my attempts to find it.

I ran off, falling down too many times to count. Something dark and unknown was hurting me and continues to hurt me even to this day. It was my unforgivable ugliness.

If only I had a tiny trace of her beauty! I felt such distress whenever I saw her swaying in front of the mirror, convinced for the millionth time that she looked like Hind Rustom, as so many people told her. When my grandmother would tell stories about the gorgeous *houri*, I could never imagine her as anything but a copy of my aunt, Fatima. I had my own theory about Fatima's beauty. My grandmother must have had "cravings" during pregnancy for the *houris* in the stories that her father, the *hakawati* with the wild imagination, used to tell.

Fatima was not satisfied knowing how beautiful she was. She believed in her beauty with conviction and thought of it as her salvation.

That radiant beauty of hers emanated from and reached its zenith on one spring day, and we would never experience such joy again.

Aisha and my sisters had preferred to shear off my hair because it made it easier to comb. I was on my way to my grandmother's house to help her pick some bitter orange blossoms in return for a few piasters. Halfway down the lane I heard women's voices, and the trill-like sounds of their joyful ululations. I approached the door, and the first thing I saw was the dazzling, rosy face of my Aunt Fatima. She appeared behind the shoulders of a man wearing a blue shirt who had taken hold of her hand to place a ring on her finger. Her magnetic eyes were even more beautiful than on any other day. They widened and flickered, almost devouring both the ring and the hands of the man in the blue shirt.

The blue of her eyes radiated more brightly perhaps because the color of the man's shirt was reflected in them. It was such a blue hue that would never be repeated again, and which I never saw except in the color of the sea on rare days at the end of April. Until this day, that beautiful portrait has never dimmed in my memory, despite all the pain and tears that ensued.

The women of the quarter suddenly appeared wearing their house clothes and untidy headscarves.

"*Mabrouk*…Congratulations, *Hakim*…*Mabrouk* to Fatima…to Imm Shibl…Allah, Allah. Dear Fatima, may you never suffer any bad thing…"

They surrounded my grandmother who, after letting out a lone ululation, stood there silently, as if her life's dream had come true. Fatima fell speechless, too. She cast quivering smiles around the room and repeatedly stroked the fabric of her bell-shaped "*cloche*" gown.

I was not so much interested in her dress, which appeared to have fallen from some other sky, as I was in the man in the shirt the same color as the "Nile cubes" my grandmother put in with the laundry. It was a color that resembled the end of the sea—the farthest ends my vision and my yearning could ever reach.

I moved closer and, through the legs of the guests present, watched him—his face, his eyes and his thin and neatly trimmed moustache. I smelled his familiar cologne—a mix of sandalwood and *ood*. He looked over at me despite my tininess. That glance was the most splendid thing that ever happened to me.

He let go of the hand of his charming bride whose hair was rippled with streaks of gold and copper, and lowered himself, bending his knees, to an ugly little girl with short hair…

"Is that you, little troublemaker? Have you been falling off the *tercina* in my absence?"

He searched for the scar to see his own creation. He smiled with satisfaction and went back to his fiancée.

It was him. No one was called "*Hakim*"—Doctor—but him. No one possessed such kindness, but him. And no one deserved my beautiful aunt but him.

He was the most handsome young man in the village and the most educated. He would become a "big time" doctor in just a few years, as his mother—the "daughter of wealth and fame"—would say, and about whom it was said, she used what she inherited from her father years earlier to buy her own handsome husband. The women whispered amongst themselves about her absence that day, but I didn't understand. And nor did I care.

I sat mesmerized on the cement floor of the room watching the young couple. My grandmother served the guests the candy-coated almonds and *baklava* that the groom's father had brought with him.

I was tasting *baklava* for the first time and witnessing my first engagement ceremony. I was also seeing clearly, for the first time, the man who had sewn up my wound and saved me from death—the beguiling man who had left his scent between the stitches on my neck.

Throughout the time when the *Hakim* would come from Russia for summer vacations and long holidays, my aunt would head to her friend Tahani's grim house daily. This was because Tahani's balcony overlooked the entrance to the Hakim's house, as opposed to our balcony which overlooked the sea.

The young girls didn't like to congregate facing the sea despite the breezes being gentle and the views captivating. Instead, they were fond of Tahani's balcony. And despite her wrath and her envy, Tahani would welcome their visits and exploit the opportunity to stay out on the balcony without raising her parents' suspicions.

Tahani would turn the cassette tape over to hear Abd el-Halim repeat his crooning over some sweetheart or other, while the young women swayed, moved by every "Ah" he uttered or kept to himself.

Fatima started telling them about how the *Hakim* had helped her niece, and how he had started ordering her to bring him this or that, and to sterilize her hands, and to calm the little girl down. They were listening and agonizing over not having been there with her, or instead of her, so much so that one of them smacked her little brother—who had followed her like a chaperone as per her parents' goading. "It wouldn't be so bad if you took a fall and broke your neck," she berated him, "so we could bring the Hakim for you!!"

They burst out laughing, with envy of Fatima burning in their hearts, for they knew that the most beautiful one among them had no competition. They hoped, whenever a suitor came for Fatima, that she would accept, so they could be rid of the one big obstacle on own their path to marriage.

Abu Mahmoud—the *Hakim's* father—held the same opinion. He was the one who had sent a telegram to his son telling him to interrupt his studies and to come and ensnare Fatima with a ring and a gold pound.

Abu Mahmoud had been setting up a trap for the moles in his garden, midway down the lane leading to my grandmother's house. It was then that he saw Abu Kamel leading a throng of his relatives on his way to ask for Fatima's hand for his eldest son, Kamel.

Not only was Kamel an engineer, but he was handsome, owned his own house, and his father was in commerce, too. Abu Mahmoud considered him a strong rival. He rushed to his wife, who had always opposed her husband's wishes to become related by marriage to my grandmother the "bedsheet launderer," as she called her. He told her that, if they didn't find him a girl to marry who is more beautiful than all the Russian girls, has a good character, and is someone we've known since she was a child, their son might end up marrying some Russian girl "whose father we have no clue about or where he came from".

That description fit my aunt to a T.

The Hakim's mother gave in but on condition she would never step foot in the bride's house.

Until today, no-one can be sure if the *Hakim* was in love with Fatima as much as his father was infatuated with her.

"You only have to look at the engagement dress that Abu Mahmoud bought for her to see that," I kept saying to the neighbor women in subsequent years. My grandmother rejected my insinuations and would say, "He adored Hind Rustom, God rest his soul. Why do you think he named his daughter Hind?"

What man did not adore Hind Rustom! Practically all of them did. But the Hakim's father probably wished to have a bride for himself like the one he had gotten for his son. The ugliness of his wealthy wife was clear proof of my suspicions.

Likewise, the whole secret behind the "*cloche*" gown was how it suited Fatima's figure so well that it seemed to have been designed especially for her. How could Abu Mahmoud have guessed Fatima's measurements with such precision!

When he left with the groom-to-be, I saw them out myself, not just with my eyes as my aunt did, exerting great effort to contain her excitement and great joy, and to maintain the haughty image she had built of herself in front of everyone.

I walked with some other children who had been bickering over the candy-coated almonds, following the groom in the hope of being treated to some more candy. But no-one in the groom's household handed out any candy. My eyes stayed glued to the blue shirt until he was swallowed up by the gate and the plump loquat fruits.

The *Hakim* went inside with his father and brother and shut the door. Then came the sounds of shouting and an argument of some sort before my grandmother passed by. She was on her way to the market to buy supplies for the next day's lunch—to which she had invited her daughter's fiancé.

She called me to accompany her and help carry the groceries.

It was a sudden engagement, so Aisha did not attend and neither did any of our relatives. But news of the engagement had gotten to the village ahead of my grandmother, and not just at the marketplace. She received dozens of congratulatory greetings and told anyone who asked the story of how the engagement had to be rushed because the groom needed to travel. There was something chirping in her throat as she spoke.

We bought meat and vegetables, spices and roasted nuts. Then, to make the *Shish Barak*, we approached the woman who sells goat milk yogurt. Fortunately, goat yogurt was in season as it was spring—the season for all delicious things, for tasty fruits and others that are sour. The bitter orange tree my grandmother planted in front of the house was ablaze in its brilliant whiteness and, as its fragrance meandered through the whole quarter, it seemed as though all the trees were brides dressed in white in the midst of their own annual wedding celebration, just like my aunt who never once renewed her own celebrations and who, for a reason that still confounds the entire village, never got married to the *Hakim*.

***

I stand before the mirror, my skin now dry and my hair, too, for the most part. It is not easy for me to feel connected to the image reflected in the mirror. It is not a familiar face I see. While Suha was plucking my eyebrows with a set of fine tweezers and a thread, it became clear she disapproved of my ignorance of my wide eyes! For her, the matter was simple. "We'll raise the eyebrows higher so the eyes will look bigger and wider."

I wipe the steam from the bathroom mirror to see I no longer resemble my father so much. So hard had I wished for that in previous periods of my life only to have it cause me pain now because no one would remember my father if they didn't see him in my face.

They would always say, "God rest his soul," whenever they noticed the resemblance between us. They would say kind words that broke Aisha's silence. But I don't blame her. Rather, I feel it was intentional he had not left a trace of himself behind. Despite my numerous attempts, I never found anything but a worn-out photograph of him which I keep in a notebook somewhere. At least I have something concrete to remember him by, while Aisha keeps only the abstract features of a man running from himself.

I remember the live birds he used to bring, to cheer me up and revive my poor health, though I would find most of them dead in the morning. I used to blame Aisha without any proof. My heart was my guide, exactly as Layla Murad used to say, whose songs blared from a small television in Aisha's shop where I was forced to stay on winter days.

The rain was waltzing around outside and, like a mirage, it was as if Layla was dancing with a man made of rain. I used to think that the person behind the mask dancing with her was my father. The shop didn't have a window or even a small skylight like most of the older buildings. Aisha couldn't have known that the cause of my illness was that shop. None of it was my fault. The kind of hair I had was not my fault—my hoarse voice was not my fault, nor my thick eyebrows. It wasn't my fault I had a sickly constitution or that I resembled my father who she hated to see or remember. Or perhaps for some reason she'd simply forgotten, because no one ever asked her about it, as if they all concurred with her hatred of him and encouraged her to it.

On days when it wasn't raining, I collected unique pebbles from the area surrounding the shop. My passion for them would be driven by a flash of their shiny marble in the distance. Pebbles that made a resonant clicking sound gave me a brief feeling of pleasure. And there, I experienced the gratuitous evil of humankind for the first time when a boy who was three years older than me approached me and said, "Poor girl, you don't have a brother or a father. It's okay. Look. I'll show you something you've never seen before." He pulled down his baggy shorts, and I was struck by the smell that overpowered me. Before any image came into view, and before I could react to it, I saw a large hand grab the pebbles there beside me and start pelting the boy with them.

It was some passerby who took me by the hand and frogmarched me to my mother. He didn't give her the details of what happened, but he did chide her and warned her not to leave me alone.

How I wished there was a small amount of goodwill between Aisha and me, so I could ask her about that man. To this day, I still don't know. Even when she got sick and grew weak, I didn't ask her.

Later on, I would sense when evil people came near. I feel I can smell them the way a cat can smell sardines. That smell which my nose was never wrong about exuded from them. The smell from between the legs of that boy with the baggy shorts.

***

I rub almond oil over my body, knowing it will make me sweat even more.

I try to turn the air conditioner on, praying that it will work if only for half an hour, until the repairman comes. But just pleading with it doesn't make it work. I settle for the fan and plop down on the bed, hugging my pillow. Feelings of estrangement and homesickness wash over me. A single teardrop is absorbed into the cotton of my familiar pillow which I brought with me, fully convinced that my sleepless hours were going to be especially long in Beirut. When I take comfort from its feel and its smell, I curl up, foetal, like an infant, and I say the sentence I've grown accustomed to saying before going to sleep.

"*Sittee*…Grandma…. Tell me a story."

Her voice comes to me from behind the walls baking under a hostile sun.

"*Kaan ya ma kaan*...Once upon a time, my dear listeners, we'll talk a little bit more and then we'll go to sleep. Once there was, in a house *faaar* far away, at the *faaar* end of the village over there, was a woman who could not have any children. She lived all alone, with no children and no riches. And on the night of *Laylat al-Qadr* (The Night of Destiny) she prayed, saying:

"Lord send me a child to raise that will fill me with joy. Send me anything, even if it's a chicken!"

God heard her prayers, and the next morning she found a little red hen at her door! Every day, the woman would watch the young girls heading out to pick wild dandelions and greens from the fields, and she would sigh with grief because her daughter was a chicken, not a girl like them. And one day, the chicken picked up a knife and a sack and followed after the girls to harvest greens with them. And when she returned, she was carrying the fullest sack of all, filled with swiss chard, purslane, wild thyme and mallow—more than all the girls!! She started going out every day to pick wild greens and would come back happy as could be. But one day, the little hen reached the king's garden and there she removed the chicken cloak and appeared out from under it as a *houri* whose beauty and loveliness no eyes had ever seen before. The chicken had been hiding in her clothing, as they say. Could she be a *jinni* princess—*Bismillah al-rahman al-rahim*—one of the King of the *Jinn's* daughters? Her face was like a slice of the moon, her hair like gold and jasmine, and her fingers like *malban* candy. And she wore ten rings, on each finger, a ring of a different size with a different jewel. She took them all off, placed them on the edge of the pool, and dove in. About an hour later, she came back up and started putting the rings on, but she discovered one ring was missing. She started counting her fingers: "This finger has a ring, and this finger has one, and this finger has one…but this finger, why doesn't it have one?" She started counting again, but again, one finger remained without a ring. Hearing some movement, she put on the chicken cloak, picked up her sack and her knife and went back to her mother. There was someone who had seen her at the pool and had been watching her. He was the one who took the ring. But who was he?"

I would beat my grandmother to the answer, peering at her in the dark. "The prince."

Eventually, the prince burns the chicken cloak so she will stay in her human form and he can marry her. Exactly like the tomcat who kills the mama cat's kittens so she will marry him.

My grandmother continues the story and then finishes it with a sad ending.

"She sat on the edge of the pool, put her children in her lap and said to her husband, the prince, "Bye-bye now," and dove into the water." And because the story doesn't have a happy and peaceful ending, I ask for another story. She scolds me and orders me to repeat after her. "*Naam ya 'abdu Allah, il-ittikaalu 'a Allah*" (Sleep now, servant of Allah, Trust belongs in the hands of Allah). And so, I repeat, "*Naam yaa Abdallah, ittikaalu 'a Allah*," (Sleep, O Abdullah, Whose trust is in *Allah*).

That is how I used to understand the sentence. I imagined we were asking the child whose name was Abdullah to go to sleep putting his trust in Allah. I didn't know at the time the servant of Allah was me and that my grandmother was herself.

I would fall asleep quickly in her bed. Her thinning hair that exuded the scent of olive oil soap and wood tar, and her clothes perfumed with wild thyme, sumac, and basil, made me feel safe. I would nod off quickly before being pummeled by Aisha's threats and curses.

"I hope to bury you! I hope you go blind! May your heart be smitten with blindness!"

Blindness and death. I didn't know which was more terrifying. They were one and the same.

That supplication echoed in the little valley and the dry brook all night long, mingling with the barking of stray dogs and the jackals that raided all the chicken coops on the outskirts of the village.

I would hear her repeat it whenever she spoke to anyone about me. "May she go blind! I told her to go get the bread, but what did she do—may she go blind—she went and fell asleep and didn't bring it. May God blind those eyes of hers. She is so exasperating!"

But something would pull me out from that nightmare. Do I have a guardian angel? A childhood demon? A fortuneteller? Or am I the daughter of the ghoul, the girl whose two sisters throw her into the ghoul's well for him to eat, but he adopts her instead and dunks her in the magic pool, and she comes out with splendid beauty, shimmering in the sun like a golden disc. Then she marries the prince and has his child, and she inherits from the ghoul after he dies. She acquires everything in the end, even things she never wished for.

I was the heroine of every story my grandmother told. I always believed that she composed them for my sake and tailored them to comfort me, until one day when she said that she learned the stories from her father—the neighborhood *hakawati*.

In an effort to show respect to the Palestinian woman, Umm Hassan, she would hum the traditional tune that Umm Hassan's ancestors sang at funerals for men from the village who had been killed in Palestine, in the 1930s, for stealing, which said, "Sigh, O Palestine… and may your men remain blackened with anger." Their anger was warranted because their best men were being killed in Palestine while selling textiles, which were being manufactured and woven in abundance in our village and all over the whole mountain.

They carried the textiles from the village to Palestine, Syria and Jordan, raking in gold pounds that got them through the winter. Her father also carried "goods"—that is, cloth garments—and traveled to Palestine, but he was spared by the highway robbers. In fact, he came back with a copy of *Alf Layla—A Thousand and One Nights*, and despite his not being very good at reading, he accepted the gift from a Palestinian man who sensed his talent for storytelling. He in turn gave the book to one of his educated relatives to read to him, and he was able to memorize the most prominent stories on the first reading.

My grandmother learned the stories by heart because they were all her father ever gave her. She didn't even inherit from him the thing that distinguished him and her brothers most of all: long thighs and arms, which were out of proportion with the back and feet. I made that observation when looking carefully at the male and female offspring of that family. I often imagined that if my maternal uncle Shibl had lived, he would have resembled my grandmother's male siblings. That dominant gene—long bones—was inherited by most of the males in the family. And this trait, particularly when it came to her younger brother, made him look very strange because his long arms were not proportional to his height and his waist, so his hands dangled at the bottom of his torso in a repulsive way.

I was afraid of him because of his shape. I didn't stare at him shamelessly—as my aunt accused me—when he came to visit us. Rather, his lanky arms and legs and gigantic hands frightened me. How could my aunt not notice that? How could she not see how he would swoop down with his hand on a fried egg and eat the entire yolk in one bite?

If we had been given a brother, he would have resembled my grandmother's father and brother. That was an unfulfilled wish my heart did not grieve over, for many other reasons, too.

***

So often had I wished that my grandmother would do nothing but tell me my stories, which I forgot as soon as I crossed over from one time period to another.

The moment the prince burns the chicken cloak, it is his own fate that is transformed, not hers. She is a magical *houri*, after all, and she will get her ten rings back and her feathery cloak, and she will sit by the same pool, sit her two children in her lap and disappear in the blink of an eye. I wished so long and hard for that chicken to be me, and for there to be no doubt that I would turn into a *houri* one day and dive towards another, better and more welcoming world. Otherwise, there was no justice in this world, and there would be no use to this life at all.

Tomorrow, when I go to the hairdresser and put on the new dress, will I change from the chicken I was for thirty years into the *houri* who will sit across from you at the dinner table and present her ten rings to you?

Tomorrow, a curse that has accompanied me since birth will cease to be, and the wounds of the past that time has not cured will be healed. Indeed, those wounds only festered from the postponement and impossibility of our meeting.

If you come and this meeting takes place, will I have something to live for?

Am I not cheating you by hiding my past and my ugliness? Is it not a wicked deception for you to see me this way? While I have never for a single day been the girl that is standing in front of the mirror right now?

Deception is not my intention. What I want is to get out of my skin, to be another person, to speak in a new way and walk in a different way.

I strap on the white high-heeled sandals to gain some height and elegance.

I walk around the room, imagining your arrival. I open the door and make way for you to enter. I trip and take a tumble in my new shoes. The almond oil has made slipping easy.

I fall on my face—exactly as I fell in your room one distant day in the past and started getting good at dreaming.

I call the repairman whose number I got from the building concierge. He says he will come late in the evening or early in the morning because he has "catastrophes" to deal with at some clinics and childcare centers. His excuses shut me up even though most likely he was lying.

All sorts of issues stir in my chest, but I possess the ability to bear them.

I will entertain myself with stories that don't lessen the harshness of this heat. My own stories, my grandmother's stories, a story with you as the hero. And I think that now is the right time to make the *mughli* pudding.

***

Why don't I feel at ease?

I circle around myself twice, searching for whatever it is I am missing. Then I remember.

The *"amta"* scarf. I don't feel free inside the house without it.

With the patience of a capable village woman who is proud of what she owns, my grandmother taught me how to put on the *amta*. I take the square of soft cloth and fold it diagonally, turning it into a triangle. I place its base over my forehead and gather the two edges together above my neck. I tie it and knot it twice. I cannot imagine myself inside the house without that little scarf. It makes me feel at ease, gives me peace of mind, makes me feel that I am free to move about among the plates and the food without fear of my hair falling onto them, and that I am an adept granddaughter, graceful, that I "do things right the first time," without going back over anything or having to fix a mistake.

An almond-shaped *kibbeh* ball gets formed perfectly in my hands in less than a minute. "Each one is the twin of the other," the neighborhood women used to say in awe, unable to tell them apart, as though they'd come out of a mold.

They ask me how I do it and how I learned, but I don't have an answer because I don't know the rules governing it.

"She learned all by herself," my grandmother says proudly, but the truth is that they taught me. I used to watch them carefully and mimic them. I would insert the long corer into a *zucchini* and in one go, I could extract all its inner flesh, leaving a layer thick enough to withhold the rice that would swell up as it cooked inside it. When I pass my knife over vegetables, I feel as though they submit to my will and become what I want them to be—meek and pliant. Some of the neighborhood women would seek me out to chop vegetables, especially for *tabbouleh*—those had to be chopped very finely and as quickly as possible—which was what my knife did best in their opinion. They would ask to borrow it, but it didn't work for them the way it worked for me. Truly, they were amazed at what I could do with that knife!! The two of us were in perfect harmony, and each one knew exactly how to please the other. I didn't work with anyone but her, and she didn't work with anyone but me.

My cooking agility wasn't just a natural-born talent. I practiced it a lot.

During those hours when I ran away from school—where I was subjected to a level of mistreatment that nearly drove me insane—and because not one girl wanted to play with me, I used to play "house" all by myself. It was after I'd given up my pebble-collecting hobby for good. I would pretend to be the lady of the house and of all the houses in the game. I played all the parts—my own role and the roles of girlfriends that I was never lucky enough to have. The only thing about playing this "house" game that was enjoyable to me was the cooking. Cleaning, sweeping and mopping were not fun things to do, and nothing ever happened while doing them. One substance didn't transform into another as it did with cooking. The matter astonished me and still does—to see ingredients added in succession, on a specific timeline and under specific conditions, to some water or oil over some sort of fire, transforming into a masterpiece!

I used to stuff mulberry leaves with clay to practice rolling grape leaves. My slender fingers helped me create a huge quantity of them. I would knead sand and pile it up like balls of dough, and then I would press down on them and make them into pancakes. Out of soft clay, I would make eggplant-shaped balls and put them out in the sun. When they dried out, I would steal my grandmother's corer and practice coring them quickly so I would be the fastest one in the quarter.

Being fast appealed to me because it was the quickest way to the women's hearts. They used to race to be the first to finish housework, despite there not being anything important awaiting them for the remainder of the day. I wanted them to talk about me, so I would stop being insignificant as I was in the eyes of my sisters and Aisha and the teachers at the "Girls' School" and all the girls, too, including Salam who eventually became my companion though not my friend.

I never made a new friend a single day in my life. Not because I was the oldest girl in my class and sat at the back of the row in the last desk, and not because I was poor, but because I had cracked and chapped hands and feet. They were repulsed by the thought of touching me.

They would mock me, relentlessly. "Do you have a bottle of orange blossom water? What's the price of soap today?"

They made fun of me because I would go house to house with my grandmother selling the products that we made and profited from.

I acted as though I didn't notice, but when I got back home, I would quarrel with my grandmother and hold her responsible for my misfortune.

But childhood was easier than what came next. It might have been a picnic compared to the hard labor prison they call "puberty".

When my panties and my apron got stained by menstrual blood, the girls pinched their noses and claimed to be nauseated. The teacher expelled me from class. She told me to go to the headmistress, but I didn't dare.

I stood at the door of the school, not knowing how I could go out like that.

The rain kept tapering off and becoming drizzle, before returning with full force. I was so miserable that I didn't notice the menstrual pains assaulting my back and stomach.

Could I disregard the pain and make a run for it before the downpour resumed?

It was cold with the ground muddy, and I was spotted with red. I stayed there trembling from cold and disgrace until the headmistress saw me and lent me a long shirt.

I went back to school after being absent for a whole week, hoping they would have forgotten what happened. But it was something that doesn't get forgotten.

I tried to concentrate and put forth my best efforts, to irritate them and also so I wouldn't have to stay back in the same grade and have girls younger than me treat me like a germ.

But I flunked for the second year in a row. I couldn't concentrate. Now I am able to tie the strings together. I understand how the changes in my body affected my frame of mind and my ability to concentrate. My incessant bleeding and staining my clothes and bed with menstrual blood, my bawling while stuck in the "water closet" thinking how to get hold of a clean sanitary napkin…and then the explosion between Aisha and me and our final battle.

I wasn't stupid, perhaps just a slow learner and, because I saw things in a different way, I took more time than all the other girls.

What vexed the schoolteachers was that I never got past my first mistakes. Year after year, in Arabic, I continued to confuse 13 with 31, left with right, 2 and 6. They said I was "stubborn" and stupid and that I was doing it on purpose.

The only thing that tempered their pursuit of me was that I was ugly. On the battleground of attractiveness and femininity, I was nowhere to be found.

My grandmother was the only person who didn't see me as ugly. She didn't say I was pretty, but she denied I was the opposite of that.

"Why am I like this, *Sittee*?"

"What do you mean, "like this"?"

"Like this…beastly…"

"Hey! What do you mean, "beastly"? Where did you get that word from?"

"They all say it…and say that I know I'm beastly… but why doesn't anyone like me?"

"Come hear this, everyone! What a shameful morning! Who hates you?"

"It's enough your daughter hates me."

"My daughter? My daughter's an idiot who has no clue where God has put her on this earth. She sits there in that shop while the customers confuse her into making mistakes. She's always bankrupt. If she wants to do laundry, she spends the whole day doing laundry, and if she cooks, she burns the food and ruins the pots. From day one, if she wanted to peel a potato, she'd peel off half the potato with the skin. She complains so much it makes a person's head spin. God gave your father some rest when He took him. Don't respond to her. Sleep over here with me tonight."

I would stay at her house and sleep in her bed. I wouldn't finish the story, not because I was still memorizing it, but because I was tired from the weight of thinking about my unknown mother, who left me at the door of the mosque, as I heard one of the girls say to my sisters one time.

"That little girl doesn't seem like she's your sister! Where did you get her from? Did you find her at the door to the mosque?"

As for my sisters, whenever I didn't serve them as they wished, they would say that a beggar woman left me on the doorstep. They didn't use the word "foundling" because they'd never heard of it, but I learned it later from television.

I also learned later just how evil I am.

I discovered the vicious evil in my heart the day I intentionally thwarted our neighbor Zaynab's plan, who, years after the engagement had been called off, wanted to bring my aunt and the *Hakim* together in a meeting that would appear to them as a coincidence. Zaynab was the only one who dared retie the broken bonds, as a kind of tribute to my grandmother, "the broken-hearted," as she described her.

In a way, I broke my grandmother's heart completely.

***

"The unexpected heatwave continues to dominate the eastern Mediterranean basin region with a slight increase in temperatures expected in the coming hours…and we remind viewers of the breaking news we reported a short time ago that a number of forest fires have broken out…"

Tomorrow might be worse than today. Perhaps the high temperature and raging sun will prevent you from leaving your hotel or your friend's apartment. Maybe the appointment will dissolve and leak out of your memory. Or perhaps you've gone to a mountain resort or are spending your day swimming in the sea.

The scenes of beachgoers on television are frightening, something akin to our parents' and the religious schoolteachers' descriptions of the "Day of the Dead." Throngs of naked people…are you among them?

On this day in early April, all those pale bodies

emerged into the sun and the stripping competition got underway. Modest bathing suits openly declare what they're carrying, and panties have a hard time hiding private parts. Embarrassed, I change the channel even though I am watching alone; it's the same embarrassment I feel when I pass by lingerie shop windows. It bewilders me how anyone can have the courage to make a naked mannequin and put a dot in the middle of each breast! I pass through the street confused, stumble over the tiniest pebble and wonder to myself, "What use is a nipple on a plastic mannequin? And how can the salesperson in such a shop be a man? How would any woman dare ask him the price of underwear or a brassiere? And how would he ask her about her bra size, and how could she answer?"

Buying underwear has always been embarrassing to me, even as recently as yesterday. I won't go into such a shop unless the salesperson is a woman. And I would never have been able to buy what I needed with peace of mind if Nabiha hadn't come up with that brilliant idea—to open a small lingerie shop—prompted by my own idea and that of the village women and their daughters that they would feel more comfortable with a female salesperson, just as they started to prefer female doctors, hairdressers and even dentists.

The day I leaned back in the dentist's chair and submitted myself to his control, I felt a knife in my heart.

"What a predicament!" I thought, while holding my breath. How can I allow a man to come so close to me and poke his fingers around in my mouth and exhale his heavy breaths onto my belly! Will this tortuous session ever end? He thought I was tensing up out of pain, but my pain was of a different sort, difficult for others to grasp.

I wished at that time that Samira—Umm Najib's daughter-in-law—hadn't moved away. Her leaving the country meant the neighborhood had lost its provider of free baby teeth extraction, and it also lost those mother-and daughter-in-law battles that were famous for being so malicious.

There was nothing more galling to Umm Najib about her daughter-in-law than her bad cooking. In one of Umm Najib's brainwashing sessions about a year before Najib left, she blamed her son saying, "Don't you ever wish you could eat a meal that isn't burnt for once? You know, come home from work and find that the soup isn't slimy?" He evaded her by quoting a popular adage, "As my grandfather would say, 'No matter what his dim-sighted wife cooks, the husband eats his dinner.'" Umm Najib was infuriated because Najib walked off and didn't hear her witty comeback. "That was in your grandfather's day. Women used to go bleary-eyed at night. But now, thank goodness for electricity!"

The various episodes of the disagreements between Umm Najib and her son didn't last long. He left for Germany and then sent for his family later, depriving generations of villagers of free molar extractions.

My uncle punched the village dentist, who had inherited the occupation from his father, the village circumciser. My aunt on my father's side had complained to her husband that the dentist pinched her cheek, so her husband broke the dentist's hand. That made them even.

The neighborhood women felt sorry for the dentist. They testified to his "decency" and high morals. But I never once empathized with a man. Even you, when you came back after your father's death and word spread about how you embraced his picture and wept with regret because he died in your absence. I didn't feel sorry for you. That was what you wanted—to get away from everyone and especially those who needed you.

I remember well what men are up to whenever I see a watermelon or smell one. That scorching summer evening when I was collecting payment for my grandmother from one of the families that resided in the oldest section of the village. Farida, the family's eldest daughter, brought a long watermelon and cut it in half, or maybe she just sank the knife into it and it appeared to me that it split in two on its own. She went about cutting "spears" of watermelon, intentionally avoiding the heart of the watermelon. In the end it was left on its own, as though it were the heart of a flower that had lost its petals. At that point she called to her father, "Dad, come have some watermelon."

Her father came and didn't pay me any heed. He leaned over the watermelon heart and started eating it without noticing the juice running down his elbows.

Here was a father who loved the heart of the watermelon and wouldn't eat any other part so, without question, his family had to leave the sugary and delicious heart for him. Maybe Farida noticed my disapproving looks and gave me the money plus a slice of watermelon, so I would leave.

***

The weather forecast on television for tomorrow shows a high of 39 degrees Celsius. Such a high temperature this time of year has not been recorded in decades.

Tomorrow 39.

Tomorrow.

"*A ghadan alqaak*? Will I meet you tomorrow?

Oh, how my heart fears my tomorrow

Oh, how I burn with longing

Waiting for the appointed time…"

I raise the volume on "Souma" (Umm Kulthum) while I prepare dinner for you. A dinner that will tell you who I am, what my story is and what I have spent my lifetime doing.

I will speak without uttering a word. Indeed, I will leave the telling of my life story to a few dishes—the one thing I have perfected in my life.

The ring of my cell phone resonates through the apartment for the first time.

Who might it be?

The concierge or the air conditioner repairman? Or you?

I look at the lit-up screen and see a number I hoped never to see. My sister Saada's number. I know that Aisha has been staying with her since she fell ill, and I know that the call is about something that Aisha wants. I try to escape it. I move away from the phone, but it doesn't stop ringing. It grows into a horrifying wailing sound. I hide the phone under the cushions in the parlor, not to be a coward but because I had claimed I was going to Damascus, so how could I answer when supposedly I don't have a phone signal?

The ringing vanishes. My heartbeat settles down. Then the notification bell rings. Saada has given up on the call and has left a message.

I dig the phone out from under the cushions and open the message.

...

That was precisely what I was afraid of—being yanked out of my happy oasis—having my heart cut in two like a ripe watermelon. All the matter required was the stab of a knife in Saada's hand.

Aisha was dying and asked to see me. How stupid is the monster who turns into an elegant and romantic young man on his death bed.

She was undergoing surgery today to remove the tumor, and the chances of survival were lower than the chances of death. I must go to the hospital in Sidon immediately, where it will be determined whether Aisha will wake up again or will sleep for eternity, taking our painful past with her. I must go, so I can get a farewell glimpse or hear the words she has waited thirty years to say.

No, no, no. I shake these thoughts from my mind.

I will not allow a fleeting moment to wipe away my entire lifetime. That is not fair. Aisha will not ask for my forgiveness, and I will not forgive her. That is not an option or something I can grant.

She's going to die.

Don't I feel sad?

I don't know.

Certainly, I am not happy. I never rejoiced over her illness since we discovered it two years ago. But I do feel a burning rage. She waited two years to muddy the most important moment of my life. She intentionally spoiled my potential happiness.

Will I let her die alone? Won't I regret that?

Wouldn't it be possible to postpone this banquet until another time? One's mother only dies once. And Aisha has chosen an unfortunate time to die—the same time I chose to live.

No surprise. We never met eye to eye a single day.

***

I look at the cinnamon-colored mixture as it boils. I search for that scene that always tries to escape me. He is my life preserver, so why does he insist on drowning? Why does he want me to forget him? I gasp and pant behind him, and I grab him.

He is the only balm for my conscience.

I relax when I remind myself the meeting between Fatima and the *Hakim* took place after Zaynab's scheme—the one I sabotaged.

I was at Salam's, sitting at the kitchen window, stirring the *mfatta'a*—rice pudding with tahini, turmeric, and pine nuts—that was simmering on the stove. It was an irritating spring day. The dust from the hill made the air in the alley heavy, and induced sneezing and itching in people with sensitive skin.

When the *Hakim* appeared in the alley, the ladle fell from my hand.

He walked toward his parents' house. And then, from the opposite direction, my aunt appeared.

They both stopped. And so did my heart.

That moment seemed an eternity of love, hatred, and pain.

His hand reached out to her, and she recoiled, as if she'd received an electric shock.

She stomped away with furious steps, leaving behind a man from her past, only to trip into another man who would sketch the contours of her dark future for her.

I came to cherish that moment later because it was the one time when we were brought together all by ourselves—just the three of us. For them it could be thought of as a unique and tragic moment together, while for me, it was a chance to spoil that idea for them.

I tried to ease my conscience. If their meeting could have fixed things between them, it would have happened that day, and not necessarily at Zaynab's. But what child could believe in such a feeble supposition?

The *mfatta'a* burned and got stuck to the bottom of the pot that day. Umm Salam lamented her luck, repeating, "We brought "Baldie" over here to entertain us!!" "Baldie" meant me.

Other things burned that day, too. I kept smelling the burnt rice and turmeric whenever my aunt surrendered to her absentmindedness, or if her silence was broken by a shudder or shiver, and I also smelled the scent of a burning heart that had thrown itself onto a hot stove.

***

I pick up the almond juices and use them to wet my thirsty pores and massage my dry skin. I rub almond oil over my body again. I want you to discover all the tenderness I have stored up for you when you shake my hand.

The feel of my skin is comforting. It reminds me of the moment of delight that floods over me every time I use caramelized sugar to remove body hair. Not just from the sugar, but from the drops of lemon juice that we add to the sugar syrup, too.

When I made the sugar to wax with yesterday, I felt as though I'd forgotten how much to put of each ingredient. Ever since I arrived in Beirut, I've been confused. I don't have any memories here, and I won't have any dreams. I even forgot my own walk. I tried to invent a new walk for myself that shows confidence, but the result came out to the contrary. I've started tripping over the dust on the sidewalk.

That was the millionth time I made the caramelized sugar, but I got flustered.

I got confused after never getting confused before, even when I made it for the first time, and despite all the neighborhood women being there at the time.

The first time is never forgotten. For everything. Even making caramelized sugar out of sugar, water, two drops of lemon juice, and a dash of saliva.

Umm Najib's granddaughter had ruined the batch, and the smell of burnt sugar filled the place. The women laughed at her, and I joined in with them. It felt good to be the mocker for once. I felt like one of those girls at school who always mocked me. I even strutted about like them, with malice and self-confidence, and I did something that my quiet demeanor had never suggested I had within me—I fixed the sugar wax.

I was ten years old. News of my sugar-making skills spread, and the neighborhood women started seeking me out to make it for them. They would spread the sugar wax over their legs and arms, filled with astonishment and delight, saying it was just right. Light-colored and shiny, pliant without sticking to the skin or melting too quickly.

On the eves of *Eid al-Adha*, *Eid al-Fitr* and wedding celebrations, I would be filled with joy because so many women would need me and ask me to come over.

I didn't like going to other people's houses, but I did like the women to need me and ask me to make the sugar for them.

I accepted every invitation no matter the circumstances. I even fought with my grandmother over it one time, when *Eid al-Adha* happened to take place on a stormy day. She warned me not to go out, and when I didn't respond, she screamed at me, "People needing to bury their dead mothers and fathers wouldn't go out in this weather. What will you get in return for making sugar wax? If you get sick, who's going to look after you? My back is killing me and I'm not up to making hospital visits!"

But I went out anyway, and I made the caramelized sugar for *Hajji* Hamda's daughters. I heard their chatter and their commentary booby-trapped with secret words. I returned home with some candy and a dress the *Hajji* didn't need. I couldn't make out its original color. The passing of time had turned it grey. It was of a lightweight fabric and smelled of mothballs. I wasn't upset that she had given me a summer dress in the middle of winter, but that she had said as she tossed it into my lap, "Here, take this. I was going to throw it away."

Despite feeling hurt, I didn't dare leave the dress behind. I took it with me.

I threw it down at my grandmother's doorstep, wiped my feet on it, and went inside. If I hadn't done that, there was no way I would have been able to sleep that night.

The next morning, I poured my heart out to my grandmother, but she didn't expound on *Hajji* Hamda's meanness. Her concern was somewhere else. "She wouldn't even give someone a hair from her butt!! What do you mean she gave you a dress?! Hand it over. I'll wash it and wear it. No matter if you put it on the doorstep! Who cares! I'll scrub it by hand, give it a good wash and wear it."

I smiled at her peculiarity and at the evil idea that popped into my mind. The next time I prepare sugar wax for *Hajji* Hamda's daughters, I'll spit in it secretly and chuckle when I see them chomping on it. That's after I add sesame seeds to the leftovers and hear them praise the "sesame candy" I'd made.

Less than a month went by before my idea was put into practice. And I also burst out laughing whenever I saw my grandmother wearing that dress.

***

My apologies to the manicurist, but I am not good at working with gloves on. These polished nails can go to hell, French manicure and all.

"French?" she had asked me. I didn't understand but nodded my head, anyway, waiting to find out what this "French" business was all about. It turns out to be the most elegant and delicate style. I liked it because it required precision and a lot of time, like a gourmet dish.

The white of the French manicure dips into the red soil, as I even it out around the stalks of the basil and mint plants. I will cut some leaves from them for the raw *kibbeh* tomorrow and remember to water them every two hours, so they won't wilt.

The idea of moving the plants from the balcony to the parlor was great because their fragrance circulated throughout the place. I was intentionally trying to change the smell of the apartment, so I scattered some thyme onto napkins and put them in every corner. And I put some orange-blossom water in demitasse coffee cups. That way, I could get rid of the smell in the house that belonged to people I didn't know. Maybe I could become familiar with this place where I would welcome you tomorrow. Tomorrow. *Ghadan*. Oh, Souma! If only tomorrow would not come, so I could go on dreaming of his arrival!

***

"If only tomorrow would not come, so I could go on dreaming of his arrival." Those words got noted in the diary I always keep with me in the kitchen.

I've always believed that great ideas come to me while I am cooking.

Whenever an idea would come to me, I promised myself to write it down after I finished cooking. But how quickly it would evaporate from my mind! That's why I decided to keep a notebook and pen in the kitchen for making quick notes until I could copy my ideas into a neat and clean notebook later. It's no surprise I have never copied a single useful sentence from that grease and sauce-stained notebook. If those ideas had truly been so great, I wouldn't have forgotten them.

When I was thirteen, I wrote my first poem in the kitchen, and I wrote it down before drying my hands:

Yes, I love you, Yes…
I love you voraciously and am not embarrassed to say, Yes
Yes, I love you, Yes.

Of course, now I am embarrassed by that prattle, but it's the poetry of an adolescent after all. I am embarrassed about a lot of things, maybe everything, that came from that creature that was crossing over from childhood to adolescence, while filled with horror and shame. I cannot hold back my tears when I recall my adolescence. And after the passing of many years, I swear that you are the only beautiful thing that happened to me during my teenage years. And I would clarify that it wasn't purely recklessness and frivolity because my love has stayed alive until this very hour, and thanks to that love, I made the most difficult decision. I tossed over my shoulder, everything I grew up fearing, from the fires of hell and the flames of the grave, to the burning embers of betrayal.

***

Night will fall soon. That moment immediately preceding it terrifies me—apprehensive of some impending evil.

As soon as I learned to talk, they taught me the two incantations. I read them before the sun goes down.

There was only one reason why they made us afraid of the night: in their worried minds, nighttime was the theater of forbidden things. That was before scandals of a moral nature were discovered to be taking place in broad daylight, not the least of which were fornication, sexual deviance, and murder. Those who knew about such scandals covered them up and feigned to forget all about them, so as to turn them into mere fairy tales. But that never worked. Most of those shocking stories, the eccentricity of which the television stations compete to expose, have similar counterparts here. They happen now just as they happened a long time ago.

Aisha used to forbid my sisters from going outside at night, even to throw away the garbage. She used a common saying as a pretext, "If you throw away the garbage at night, you'll stop the flow of blessings into your household." I knew she was making excuses because our household was devoid of any such "blessings." And my grandmother would talk about a little girl eaten by a wolf which ate her grandmother too because, while out on her walk—without an adult escort—she had broken her parents' rules not to speak with evil strangers. And the old folks told stories about the female *jinns* who would roam freely at night, singing and dancing and chasing after men enticing them to fall in love with them.

Sundown is the time when the *jinns* come out from their hidden dwelling places.

My nephew, barely two months old, would cry hysterically every sundown. My sister became frightened and sought my grandmother's help. She set her mind at ease telling her it was natural because that was the time when the *jinns*—"*Bismillah al-rahman al-rahim*"—were passing through. They come out at the start of night because they are its masters, and we should leave the nighttime to them.

It was forbidden for us girls to go out alone because a monster standing on two legs would gobble us up. Or because the *jinns* would touch us. Christian upbringing was more merciful. A Christian colleague of mine at the co-op told me that the peak hour for the activities of demons and evil spirits was three o'clock in the morning. I joked with her, "So you can come home at two o'clock and no one says a word to you?" She laughed, pleased by this luxury afforded her.

On the nights when I stayed home with Aisha, I didn't sleep. I was afraid of nightmares. And there weren't any stories there to make me sleepy.

When the sun rose and my sisters woke up, I would turn my back to everyone and stare at the whitewashed wall, hoping Aisha would go off to the shop before I had a chance to see her. As if I were an accused criminal dreading having to stand trial.

Now I know my sin: hatred.

She would not look into my eyes when she talked to me. She searched for anything else to look at but me.

Whenever we were near each other, she would look at me out of the corner of her eye, watching me, scrutinizing me, waiting for the tiniest mistake or wrong move so she could launch an attack.

I turned to cooking as an escape. I would ignite the stove and prepare the first dish that came to mind. Whenever we were brought together in one place, I felt the weight of the air and the death of time. I imagined people arguing and fighting in the space surrounding us and in the air that was heavy with the foul words they were lobbing at each other. This was why I avoided being in the same place with her.

As the fire cooked the food, I looked into it, daydreaming, and asked myself, "Why doesn't she look into my eyes? And why does she wish for me to go blind?"

The two questions had the same answer, or one of them was the answer to the other: she wished blindness on me, so I would not look into her eyes. She had something hiding in them—something atrocious. Perhaps today she wanted to confess it to me.

The fire hurt my eyes, so I closed them.

Despite all their attempts to scare us with the idea that fire was the worst kind of punishment, I never despised it for a single day.

I love fire when it transforms whatever is in the pot into something equivalent to happiness.

Human beings light a fire and dance around it in celebration. Never once did they put out a block of ice and dance around it or smile at it, even in the hottest days of summer. Ice has no heart. But that is a simple matter. We don't have to read books to understand it.

I read many books to understand that the prophets who lived in deserts imagined hell in the image of fire. If those religions had appeared at the north pole, they would have described hell in the form of ice and snow.

Before reading those books, I used to wonder to myself—why does God have to strangle us and roast us over a flame? Isn't he merciful to us? Wouldn't he refrain from roasting us alive? Or does he sometimes strangle us, revive us, and then roast us? I asked the religion teacher once, and she said the second supposition was the correct one. God gives us new skin whenever our skin melts away, so we can burn time and time again for ever and ever.

It's true I didn't sleep for two nights after that talk from the teacher. And I never asked her about the matter again, but my grandmother told me that, if I sought God's forgiveness, he would grant it because he is merciful and forgiving.

That was everything my grandmother knew about punishment and reward for good deeds, and everything she needed to know about God—forgiveness and mercy. But, despite her putting my mind at ease, she never hesitated to threaten me, at the slightest mistake I made, "God will strangle you!"

"God will strangle you if you throw bread away. God will strangle you if you show the bottom of your shoe. God will strangle you if you play with boys. God will strangle you if you get dirt in the dough. God will strangle you if you throw the bread in the garbage can."

We had to eat the bread even if it was hard and dry. As for when it was moldy, then we had to give it to the chickens after kissing it and raising it up to our foreheads several times and begging for forgiveness. Throwing it in the garbage was ingratitude towards God's generosity.

At night, when the sound of jackals reverberated through the village, I feared that the hand of God would stretch forth and strangle me. I would hide my neck between my shoulders and feel that I was choking. I wished if only he would give me a minute to say to him, "Not with your hand, God…not with your hand…don't strangle me with your hand…I am scared to death of the idea of your hand strangling me…let me go, I will die from my fear of you. Let me go, and I will die on my own. Don't make me blind as Aisha has asked you because I am afraid of the dark."

When the ghoul's daughter fell into the well, she couldn't see her own finger even as a shadow. She groped the damp walls and nearly fainted. Just like what happened to me when I fell into the room that people say was built over the well of your house. That is not a coincidence. It is proof that we were together in some version of that story. She arrived at the ghoul's palace and hid herself in fear of him, but when he sneezed, he startled her and she cried, "Father help me!!" And so, the ghoul thought he had been blessed with a daughter. He adopted her and gave her the keys to ninety-nine of the one hundred rooms in his palace.

The ghoul's life changed, for ghouls also long for a reason to wake up each day. He started heading out on his hunting expeditions full of energy and would return clasping a cow with swollen udders around his shoulders or an entire tree, roots and all. He would give them as gifts to his daughter who would sprout up upon his return like a truffle responding to a startling stroke of lightning from the skies above. As for the "daughter of the ghoul," her goal was to break into the forbidden room. After a bitter struggle she decided she would enter it…and in she went. She saw what she had never expected to see—a pool with breadth and depth which had no end. She dipped her index finger into its golden waters, and it turned into a solid chunk of gold. When the ghoul found out, he didn't get angry. Instead, he plunged his daughter into the pool. She became such a wonder that when she did her knitting out on the balcony, the sun felt shy next to her and rushed to hide itself behind the nearest cloud.

***

I sit on the sink to stir the mixture of ground rice, sugar, cinnamon and caraway, which takes four full hours for the concoction to turn into something rare in the paradise of delicious tastes.

Four hours of boiling are what gave this dish its name: *mughli*—'boiled concoction'—a woman's companion when she comes of age and one of the intimate elements of her world.

It's not just an hour and a half. Four hours is a substantial amount of one's lifetime—one sixth of the day. And for the cook, it is exhausting work, second only to *mfatta'a* which takes six hours. My grandmother—who has never liked *mfatta'a*—says it got that name because it *tfatti' al-dulouh*, "tears apart the ribs" from so much stirring, but I believed the reason was in the forming of the dish itself. The *mfatta'a* mixture in its final stages *yitfatta' 'an baadu* "gets torn apart" like threads torn by a seam ripper, which is evidence it is finally cooked to perfection.

Ask me why women invented these time-consuming dishes. Ask, so I can answer you.

If you were here with me now, I would tell you this:

Women didn't invent it—as men like to claim—because they have so much time on their hands. On the contrary, they were busy all the time and did everything themselves—from making bread to sewing to raising chickens and making dried foods…and they also gave birth a lot and took care of numerous children.

They didn't make these dishes because they were idle, but rather to prove through them their love for whoever would eat them and come to visit the new child, and to congratulate the woman who had just given birth.

They've known for ages that cinnamon, carraway and nuts are ideal for increasing the flow of breastmilk.

"Cinnamon fills up the breast," my grandmother used to say to one of my sisters whose breastmilk was slow in coming. Cinnamon makes the nipple overflow with milk and heals the womb after its labors. It is the ideal meal for returning strength to a woman who has just emerged safely from God's hands, and it's also perfect for bringing the womb back to its original place and natural size, so it can prepare to have a new egg nestle inside it.

Why not?! Don't women always ask a woman not long after giving birth, "Aren't you pregnant with the next one yet?"

Mughli was an unequivocal act of love. They let the joy of tasting and the lavish spending on expensive nuts deliver the messages of their hearts. That's because they were brought up hiding their feelings and denying their natural impulses to the point that they were prohibited from reading at one time, so they couldn't write love letters to prospective suitors.

It wasn't just men who didn't permit girls to have an education for that reason, but also the mothers and grandmothers. It was such a loss that women did get educated afterwards and started writing letters! They had thought up such unique ways of divulging secrets and developing their cooking and desserts. They inspire me with unique methods for expressing the ardent love I have in this difficult moment I am living. It's no surprise that our kitchen remained where it was and that our cuisine remained exactly the same, passed from grandparents to grandchildren…arriving finally to me.

The two words "*beetsa*" and "*hamborgher*" ring in my ears every time a woman says them. Those two dishes will always be new, indeed forever alien to our world. The women don't exert any effort to correct their pronunciation.

I recall my grandmother's rejection of those two things with words like, "What kind of ridiculous invention is that!!" So, I would try to soften things for her. "Pizza is just cheese *manousheh* that they added some olives and tomatoes and vegetables to. And a hamburger is a round meat sandwich. That's all there is to it. No invention, no nothing."

"Okay. Give me a little taste so I can see for myself." She takes a taste and likes the pizza, but she remains reluctant. "Nothing compares to our own food. They can say whatever they want!"

The Palestinians have lived among us forever, but their *mouloukhieh* never found its way into our homes.

In fact, we continue to refer to it while refraining from consuming it as "slimy," and we don't like *musakhkhan* because it makes us run out of sumac, which we need for canning provisions for winter! We lived with and among them, and we joined our families through marriage, but cooking is another matter altogether. It's not about looking down on anyone or being racist. Perhaps it's just a question of timing. They came to live with us in the middle of the twentieth century—a period when we had gotten lazy with our efforts and developments. Maybe the political setbacks and defeats entered into our kitchens and turned creativity in cooking into a luxury that women didn't dare afford themselves. Undoubtedly, the war killed our appetite for inventiveness and stamped out the practice of rejuvenation. And so those among us who migrated tried to stabilize the situation and from their places of emigration, they took renewed interest in the cuisine of their burned-down homeland.

When she came to visit my grandmother, Mary used to show us pictures of her family—her daughter Karen and her Australian son-in-law. Most of the pictures were taken around a dinner table covered with a variety of Lebanese dishes. Mary would go on about how her son-in-law adored the Lebanese food she prepared and would turn into a ravenous child, getting oil from the stuffed grape leaves all over his hands.

Mary disapproved when my grandmother's sister married off her daughter to a young Palestinian man. Not because Mary is Christian, as many Muslims also disapproved, but because the children of that young woman would become Palestinians living in a country that did not grant them civil rights. However, even that crucial fact didn't prevent intermarriage of that type in our village, which was fairly tolerant of strangers and transients. This was possibly because our ancestors were traveling merchants who knew what it meant to "cross many roads," and early on they knew that even in their own homes and their own lands they themselves were nothing but visitors and guests.

Mary resumed praising my speed at rolling the stuffed swiss chard leaves she would take with her to Australia.

As I place the rice, tomatoes, parsley and onions in the center of the swiss chard leaf, I consider whether Mary remembers "Ooh La La!" candy, or the television station *Télé Liban*? She confirms my suspicions when she starts talking about some shows on LBC that she is obsessed with, particularly the Mexican soap operas.

I always considered my long fingers ugly. Anyone who praised them praised their skill and speed, not their beauty. But Mary lauded them saying, "You could be a pianist…if only…"

She didn't finish. If only what?

I didn't know my fingers could catch the attention of a woman like Mary. The women of our quarter used to praise my agility at rolling stuffed grape leaves, cabbage and swiss chard, but they never ever made a connection between that and playing the piano. The piano never crossed their minds or made its way into conversations in our alley. If not for songs like "*Qalbi wa miftaahu*" (The Key to My Heart) and "*Ahwaak*" (I Love You), we wouldn't have any way of knowing the piano exists.

Water, salt, garlic, cleaning detergents, working in the fields and working in the factory, all made my fingers rough. When I write, I feel them scratching against the paper. All my letters are scraped by skin that the passing days have subjected to suffering.

I would not have noticed my fingers withering away had I not been writing letters. And I would not have been writing letters had it not been for you.

I open the notebook where I keep my neatly folded letters and pick up the first one I wrote to you. I wrote that I would go to you—that I would not live anywhere except where you are. And I was waiting for you…Lots of mistakes, messy handwriting. Suddenly, I notice all the words in a circular area on the page have been erased by a teardrop. I was crying as I wrote. Rather, I was writing because I was crying. That is what happened later and continues to this day.

I was not planning to send those letters. And now I am overcome with a desire to be free of them.

You will not read them.

No one must know the person I am cooking for now is that same nasty fiancé of my aunt—the man who caused me more than one scar and caused her more than one insult. He must remain abandoned there in the alley, reaching out with his hand into the heavy void, into the painful nothingness.

I will not tell you I knew you before—that I attended your hasty engagement party—and witnessed the tears of a young woman you left, with no justification—and lived in a household that hated you as much as my heart loves you.

I will let you figure it out. I will test your instincts as a doctor, for if your heart guides you, and you recognize me or, if you merely remember my name, then the portion of my lifetime that has passed will not have vanished into nothing.

2

Late afternoon in the city is oppressive. It makes the hooting of the owl reverberate in my mind.

This is the owl's time. Perhaps, she has come to the carob tree, for spring is here, and these are the owl's days.

"The carob owl" is what everyone calls her. There's no need to tell you her seasonal story. Every single person in the quarter claims she has come at some time to target him or her—even those whose houses do not overlook the brook and who can't see the carob tree from their rooftops. They all have some story with the owl.

I will not mention her over dinner. But while you were away, we lived through some tragic times with that owl.

They shot at the owl, and so she disappeared for two whole seasons and the people of the quarter thought she had been killed. But she came back. My aunt Fatima said it wasn't the same owl, though. It was her daughter. But for some reason, I felt it was the same owl—she hadn't been hit by the bullets which rained down on the carob tree that spring night because I prayed for her not to get hurt. To just go away.

After many intense winter months, it was a beautiful warm night. The frogs' voices rose up, heralding an imminent rise in temperature. I loved to hear the frogs croaking because I hate the cold. And I didn't hate the owl. But I never had the strength to reveal that because the word itself—*boumeh*—owl—had a way of drawing signs of disgust and annoyance on everyone's faces.

When I was little, I told Salam that the owl had gotten the hiccups, and Salam believed me. It always surprised me how Salam believed everything I said, and it made me feel better knowing she was dumber than me. But I regret it now, because to this day Salam is my only friend, and the tragedy that befell her after her marriage hurt me as though it was my own tragedy.

The carob tree did not provide anything of much use. It was inhabited by bats, harmful insects and other creatures that were never spoken about in front of children.

Very early on, my grandmother warned me not to go near the carob tree at night. She said that many '*bismillah al-rahman al-rahim*'s lived in it.

I had no idea what those things could possibly be, only that they were dangerous and scary. Whenever I walked past the carob tree during the day, I would shudder. Was that the reason my aunt was in favor of cutting it down? Or was it the sound of the owl announcing an evil omen?

My aunt could not be steered away from the idea of getting rid of the tree until, stirring some chestnuts around in the little "*kanoun*" stove, my grandmother said, "Let them stay in the carob tree. Better than having them move to some other place."

My aunt's mind wandered far while my mind stayed focused on things closer to home—like the roasting chestnuts my grandmother's wrinkled fingers were turning over without any need for tongs and without being harmed by the heat, due to the roughness of her skin. The heat of the embers didn't affect anything except the scent of the orange blossom water lodged inside my grandmother's pores, which wafted delicately around the place.

Even when her mounting illnesses incapacitated her, her blood continued to exude a sweet fragrance, which, over time, had become a part of her.

When I would dry her off and dress her in cotton clothes, the scent of olive oil soap, lavender and orange blossom water emanated from her veins, as though those smells had dwelled in her for a lifetime.

In her weakened state, I would keep offering her food to prevent her being hungry at night. That way, death couldn't carry her away hungry.

That was my nightmare. For death to take her before morning came. I would feed her "Lebanese Nights" dessert, which I learned how to make for her sake.

I didn't know how to tell her I loved her or how to apologize for leaving her to sleep all alone for so many years while I slept in a refurbished bedroom up on the roof of the house. How could I be absolved for my arrogance towards her, my attempts to escape her snoring, and all my grumbling? How could I tell her that I hated myself for being ungrateful and had given in to despair after the passing of so many days in which nothing ever happened? That I never found anything positive, and didn't even feel the desire to cook for anyone?

"Just take one taste from each plate. Just give them a taste…"

She would try to evade me saying, "Don't you want me to tell you a story? Or do you think I'm old now and don't remember?"

In truth, she wasn't afraid of dying of hunger, but of dying with no memory.

She would tell the stories in bits and pieces, mix them in with other stories and change the fates of the heroes. Then she would appeal to me for help, knowing that I would be polite and wouldn't correct her.

I would tell the story so she could remember it. The dark was intense, so I couldn't see her tears, but I knew they were pooling up in the corners of her eyes.

I cried too between one sentence and the next. I would hold back my sobs so the story characters could live happily ever after.

For two and a half decades she bathed me, dressed me and put me to bed. Today, I'm not returning the favor because she never asked for anything in return. And I don't feel that I'm paying back a debt but rather that I am making amends for something I will feel guilty about later.

When, a decade and a half earlier, and filled with sorrow, she spoke about her mother being "lost," meaning she had lost part of her memory and her concept of time and place, she sat weeping over her mother as if she had actually died. The neighborhood women tried to ease her worries, but she just kept saying, "Once you're 'lost' you're three quarters dead."

She was certain about that from living around the elderly. She wasn't speaking out of distress or stupidity.

She used to wash the bedsheets and clothes for the incapacitated old folks. She would spare me from visiting them and only dragged me along if it was absolutely necessary. And she never talked about them in front of me except with a few words here and there. She always had a lump in her throat that kept a lot of things hidden. It made me imagine how they cried like children because one of their relatives didn't visit or because they'd lost control of their bowels on beds not their own or because their bones were being gnawed away by the cold and the loneliness.

When I accompanied her to the nursing home, I would stand back, afraid to go near them because their skin was covered in wrinkles, like turtle skin, and they moved slowly like turtles, too.

I didn't tell her she wasn't going to die now. I reminded her of her parents, brothers and sisters who all lived into their eighties.

I assured her she wouldn't die before reaching eighty. But life made a fool out of me.

I was sitting out on the doorstep begging the sun for some warmth at the end of winter when I heard her mourning my grandfather and singing "lamentation verses" for the dead. I knew then she was dying. I got scared and went to the kitchen to boil the sheep bones and wheat to make *hreeseh* stew that she loved so much.

***

I have a craving for *hreeseh* all of a sudden.

How could I not have thought of it? How could it have slipped my mind?! It's also a celebratory dish eaten during our wedding celebrations, but you haven't seen a single one in two decades. Although *hreeseh* is essentially a poor man's dish, a modest dish or possibly an act of deception, being one of the lowliest foods—basically wheat and bones—the grease and fat from the bones and the small amount of meat attached to them was compensation to the poor unable to afford lean meat. That was how our grandmothers came up with solutions to the problem of their children's hunger and craving for meat and fatty food.

Don't scold me for my craftiness. There is a lot of cunning in the world of cooking, such as substituting an expensive ingredient for a cheaper one, and especially at wedding celebrations that would feed an entire village.

Tomorrow is not a wedding for anyone except my eyes that will be married to your face and your tall frame. I want to stare at you for a good long time. That's never happened before. Even in my dreams which bring you before me, you disappear quickly, like a stingy flash of light. And when I wake up, the memory of your face seems even further away from me than memories of the womb, when I would fall asleep in troubled waters.

How could I forget the *hreeseh*? Is it because it is associated with funerals? I don't recall if it was served at my father's funeral, but it was there at every funeral I ever attended. I made it myself for your father's funeral, two days before you arrived. I was sad because you came late, not because I was lamenting over the deceased.

When the women ate their fill of the *hreeseh*, Umm Najib tucked the edge of her skirt between her calves, crossed one leg over the other, and in the tone of someone about to make an important declaration to an ignorant audience—meaning us—she said, "The *Metualis* make *hreeseh* at *Ashura* and share it with neighbors and relatives, supposedly in honor of Al-Husayn's soul."

Here the women knit their brows in surprise.

Umm Najib puts their minds at ease. "What's the problem? The *Fatiha* is said in honor of his soul. He is the grandson of our *Sayyidna* Muhammad, after all, which means he's a Sunni by birth! The last time I went to see my sister-in-law's family—her mother is a *Metuali*—one of their relatives there, who didn't know me, thought I was of the same denomination. I have no idea what made her start talking about us! She said we weren't clean, that we don't pour water over the clothes when we hang the laundry…they say you're supposed to water it. They grab the water jug and pour water back and forth along the clothesline!"

All the women there got worked up and started repeating like a broken record, "*We* are the clean ones! *They* do everything wrong. They say we should "water" the laundry. How ridiculous!! No wonder they're always covered in mud!"

Umm Najib laughs, holds onto the two edges of her smile with her thumb and index finger and says, "I said to my sister-in-law, figure out how much the blood money should be, so we can pay it and be done with this long overdue revenge."

***

The brown mixture has started to thicken, but it is just the beginning—the end nowhere in sight. This was why the women would gather in a circle around the pot of *mughli* or *hreeseh*—to help the hosts create a joyful occasion. They shared in both their happiness and toil. They took turns stirring and, as the big wooden ladle got passed from hand to hand, the latest news got passed along their tongues—everything from village news to neighborhood gossip to their most personal secrets—what pained them in the morning, what disturbed them in their sleep, what worried them at night, what terrified them as they performed their ablutions at dawn. They would tell it all over the cooking pot, which had become the center of their world—everything, even what they argued about with their husbands. It helped for them to look into the pot while divulging secrets. It freed them from having to look at each other and having to face the embarrassment of the other women's stares while they complained about the things that pained their souls.

One of them would curse her stepfather for whatever harm he'd caused or stinginess with which he'd treated her or her siblings. And then another woman would console her by complaining about her husband for withholding money that could be spent on his children so he could go "gamble and bet on horses." And a third woman would make them feel better by complaining about her son who was under his wife's thumb and had been at odds with her for years.

Then my grandmother would shut them all up by recalling the last conversation she had with my grandfather. "He took the gold bracelet off my wrist to go sell it and told me, 'As long as I'm alive, you have nothing to worry about,'" she says, in a disapproving tone. "He said that on Saturday and he died on Monday!! As long as he's alive. Hah!"

This "flipping over of sore spots" would be undercut by silly questions or funny questions, like the one Salam asked when she was twelve years old. "There's a question that has been bothering me! Isn't Abd el-Halim dead? How can he be singing on the radio?"

They would get in a good laugh before resuming their stories.

But I am here now all by myself, in this strange and gloomy place.

I'm not used to the layout of the apartment and for there to be a dining room across from the kitchen. And this kitchen is very strange—spacious, with a gigantic refrigerator! I am not accustomed to such luxury or for the kitchen to have a window. The proof is that I am sitting stirring the *mughli* dressed in my *shalha* housecoat. My grandmother's kitchen, in which I spent a large portion of my lifetime, was the heart of the house. There was no window exposing it to the outside, and I could prepare food wearing the least amount of clothing possible.

I jump down from the sink and look at my *shalha*. Then I hurry to the bedroom and open the closet.

All my clothes are winter clothes. When I moved them here, I wasn't expecting this sudden heatwave.

What am I to do? The only piece of summer clothing is the dress I bought to wear to our dinner. But I won't chance it by wearing it now. It could get soiled or burned. What if someone were to come now?

But who in the world would come? No one in the area knows me, and none of my acquaintances knows I'm here.

I should go right away to the store and buy something summery to wear. But I can't leave the *mughli*. It will be ruined, and I'll have to start all over again and throw this batch in the garbage. I hate to throw food away. Abandoning it now would be offensive to it and to me.

The doorbell!!!

***

I stand in my *shalha* in front of a closet that has one pair of jeans and two winter sweaters inside it. I put on whatever I grab and go answer the door, but before replying to the repairman's greeting, I run to the kitchen because the *mughli* is about to start sticking to the bottom of the pot.

My body is on fire as I yell to the repairman to come inside, apologizing that what's on the stove was about to burn. He pokes his head inside the kitchen door. He's skinny and resembles a stalk of green mint in a cup of hot tea. I tell him there are two air conditioners in the house—one in the bedroom and the other in the parlor—and that I want to move the one in the bedroom into the kitchen. His eyes pop when I say this because it will take a long time in his opinion, plus I didn't mention that on the phone.

He goes on mumbling while I drip with sweat in my winter sweater. Shall I take it off and just let whatever might happen? Will he attack me if I do that? How would I defend myself in such a circumstance?

I imagine myself throwing the pot at him. Let him "roast and burn." But then a better idea comes to mind.

"Do you get paid by the hour?" I ask him. He doesn't answer because he doesn't understand the reason for the question. "Okay, come here. Take hold of the ladle and keep stirring. This is a lot easier than moving the air conditioner. Keep stirring until I get back."

I steer him towards the burner and put the ladle in his hand. He's dumbstruck. He starts stirring involuntarily, and then he asks, "Hey, where are you going? What have I gotten dragged into?"

From the doorway, I tell him I'm going to get some very important medicine I need, and I'll be back in a flash.

At the closest shop, there are only dresses, which aren't much different from my *shalha*, which I almost had on when I greeted the repairman. I don't have time to look for another shop, so I buy a summery blouse, which I put on right away, and I also buy a lightweight dress to wear tomorrow to the coiffeur.

When I open the door, I discover that I had locked it from the outside with my key, meaning I had locked the repairman, "the wilted mint twig," inside. I feel so stupid and harmful! What if a fire had broken out inside the apartment, or there had been some sort of electrical problem, and he needed to save himself? Was he to throw himself from the fifth floor?

I see his tool bag is still where it was, and the scent of cinnamon wafts in the air, not something burning. I go into the kitchen in my new blouse and see his gaze land on my collar and chest.

I try to make things right. "*Yislamu.* Thank you. I am so grateful. God bless you. What is your name?"

"Karim."

"Ha-ha! I was going to ask, '*Shoo il-ism il-karim*'—What is your *honorable* name?"

"Nothing would have changed. I'd still be Karim."

It's clear he doesn't find me attractive. I rush to take the ladle and ask him to fix the two air conditioners and start moving the air conditioner from the bedroom to the kitchen because tonight I plan to sleep in the kitchen!

That just makes matters worse, for Karim now appears certain I am crazy. It occurs to me that he might run out of the apartment and cry for help.

But he goes right to work.

Then he speaks to me from where he is in the parlor that opens onto the kitchen—his hair soaked with sweat seems clear proof of my first impression of him—saying, "I get it. You went out to buy that blouse, not medicine."

I laugh. "Yes, you're right. How did you know?"

"It doesn't take a genius. It's obvious. No offense to your intelligence."

"If you happen to be in the area in about three hours, stop by for a bowl of *mughli*."

Prime example of village mentality! I am going to be discovered. He will find out that I am a naïve village girl and corner me. I slide the kitchen knife closer to myself.

"*Mughli*…I thought it was *mughli*, but you don't look like you just had a baby, and there's no trace of any children in the house."

"It's *mughli* without a newborn…just a craving."

"A craving in this heat! *Mughli* is hot. You'd be better off making Jell-o or maybe some ice cream."

He is right to a certain extent. But how could I make him understand what this dish means to me in the dictionary of love and affection?

Do I tell him that numerous women I know used to ask me to make the *mughli* for them after giving birth because the *mughli* that I make, according to them, is the best? Do I tell him how the thousands of bowls I've made didn't have a single bit left behind? People would gobble it up and lick the bowl. They would smack their lips, astonished that the person who had made the *mughli* was so young—not an old woman who had spent her entire life making it!

"You know what?" the repairman says. "I was afraid to leave the pot unsupervised. I said when you come through the door, I'm going to jump out the window…but…"

"Why did you change your mind?"

He stays silent for a moment then says, "The blouse looks nice on you."

The ladle shakes in my hand. No, my entire body shakes. Is this man flirting with me? Today? Am I receiving the first direct flirtation ever in my whole life? In this strange place in the middle of this heatwave? While I'm here all alone with a man I don't know, who I'm seeing for the first time?

Is he flirting with me at the same time Aisha is dying? The one who spent her whole life convincing everyone, including me, that no one would ever take a second glance at me?

I get scared.

How could a little affectionate statement both scare and silence me that way?

Karim notices my silence, so he pokes his head out the kitchen door. This is the only time I see his face clearly. I hadn't really taken a good look at him until now.

He smiles apologetically. "Sorry…don't misunderstand me…I just meant it looks nice on you…*Mabrouk*! Wear it in good health!"

I move closer to the kitchen window that overlooks the street. If he attacks me, I'll scream, and the passersby will save me.

He seems nice and good-hearted. Poor thing. He's not like those others lazing around at the beach. He is hard at work in this stifling heat. He is like me. He battles on, no matter how much the heavens persecute him. Maybe, like me, he lives waiting for signs from there, too.

He likes what I bought. What would he say about the dress for tomorrow? Should I ask him?

The idea both haunts and entices me. But I go back to my unconscious promise to you: your eyes alone will be the first to see me in the dress.

***

My heart was trembling as I traversed the streets of Sidon looking for a dress for the promised rendezvous.

The idea was dizzying in two ways—I was on the verge of buying the dress I would be wearing when I saw you and you would see me wearing.

How could I look like the princess of your dreams and look natural at the same time? Should I choose something dazzling or something simple to keep my frivolity and craziness hidden? What color do you like, and what color do you hate? What color suits me best?

The right color. That is what I wanted to figure out.

Depending on the salesmen at the shops was of no use. They like anything a customer tries on because they want to sell and don't care about what is most becoming, or if the customer is about to have an encounter with the love of her life.

Black? White? Red? Brown? Green? Blue…

I was sure about one thing: that you like the color blue. You had chosen it for the day of your engagement.

But that was more than two decades ago. They say that people's preferences change over the years. I don't give much credence to that saying, though. I am still dedicated to my crazy choice to plunge myself into your world, or at least into your past which you turned your back on and walked away from, fleeing from your fiancée or some transgression or crime. No one knows for sure.

I know one important thing, which is that if you are regretful now and yearn for what you had before, then you will find it with me.

You will find it in the perfect amount of sweetness in the *mughli*, and the balance of caraway and cinnamon, and the correspondence between the color and the flavor. You will find it in the moistness of the coriander and cheerfulness of the mint…

I know if you are missing your old memories, then you will find them between my fingers and within everything that comes out of my hands. You will find them on the tip of the tongue I use to taste what I'm cooking.

I touch the fabric of the dresses on display and wonder how life would appear if—by some haphazard step—you were to touch my dress?

Have they invented a kind of cloth that calms the soul's fears, and applies cooling and peace to a burning heart? A kind of fabric that alleviates the stomach pain, the butterflies that began to intensify the moment I stepped toward our long-awaited meeting?

Why do our stomachs hurt when we are in love? This question has bewildered me for so long. I read in philosophy books that the stomach houses sensual delight as well as weakness. It is the lower and vulgar part of a person, whereas the mind is the higher and superior part, and it controls what is below it and what is without it. Racing heartbeats coincide with pain in the stomach, and contractions are distributed in the body without a clear map. My heart contracts and then my stomach. My blood vessels and then my waist and then my stomach once again. My womb and then my lungs. As though I were a mine field. One mine going off after another.

I won't be saved.

At a shop that sells evening gowns, there was a young woman trying on a short dress, so the shop owner said to her, "My dear young lady, a short dress shortens your stature. Better to get a long one. It'll give you height and flatter your figure."

A bit of information at just the right time. A long blue one, then. This is what I'd determined to be the gown of my dreams.

I read something similar in a fashion magazine. The idea was that long hair gives the impression of extra height and makes a woman appear taller. I didn't know that when I decided, as a child, not to cut my hair. Rather, I was silently defying Aisha and dreaming that this coarse and matted hair of mine would transform one day into wavy hair like my aunts and sisters had.

My aunt was scary like her sister Aisha, but she didn't direct her anger at me.

Only later did I see why the apt description for her was "*Namroudi*," haughty and arrogant, as my grandmother called her during one of their quarrels. She had refused to wear Mary's hand-me-downs, about which the only thing I remember is how they smelled of perfume.

She justified her vanity because she was beautiful, and the "people" that she was always mentioning whenever she spoke—without specifying who they were—liked girls who had pride in themselves—the vain and unshakable ones.

Yes, she was astonishingly beautiful, and no one was more aware of that than I because I was constantly scrutinizing her, desperately trying to determine what

I was missing which could make me like her or edge closer to being like her. But I never found anything to convince me she was truly my aunt or to give me hope I'd become like her one day, which was the opposite of my five sisters. They had divvied up their aunt's captivating beauty amongst themselves. One of them got the wide eyes. Another got their stark blue color. Another got her bewildering hair—somewhere between golden and copper colored. Yet another got her marvelous figure.

My sister Suad inherited the largest share of Fatima's beauty. The two of them looked like sisters whenever they walked beside each other. And like Fatima, Suad tried to hide her feelings of inadequacy, the shame of poverty and being fatherless, but as they passed by, any person who took a close look at them caused the walls of haughtiness to come crashing down. They both knew what every young girl in the village knows—that whenever a girl passes along a street studded with curious eyes looking for imperfections, then she becomes exposed to everything, even to delving into her mind, reading her thoughts, and knowing her entire family history.

Where did Fatima get that beauty neither her mother nor her maternal aunts possessed?

Her name was the key to the secret.

She was born after a series of tragic miscarriages of male fetuses, with a boy surviving just one month and a girl who is still alive today. My grandfather refused even to look at her. He didn't congratulate his wife, but said instead, "Thank God you're okay," and left the house before he could hear her response.

He regretted it the moment he stepped out the door, but he didn't turn back to see his daughter.

A week later, he picked up the baby girl, not yet having given her a name—she was simply called "little girl," and her mother didn't dare ask her husband, "What do you want to name her?"

When he picked her up, his face brightened. He saw in his daughter a dear face he had been missing for a long time. The face of his grandmother Fatima who was famous for her stunning beauty, which none of her sons inherited. He saw light radiating from beneath her skin and predicted copper colored hair and dark blue eyes. That was why he named her Fatima, after his grandmother, with no deference to the wishes of his mother-in-law who had hoped her son-in-law would honor her after having named his eldest daughter after his mother Aisha.

My grandmother was not sad he hadn't used her mother's name. She was disappointed because she had given birth to a strong and healthy baby girl, whereas she had miscarried all the boys. That was an ailment expressed by the saying, "Boys don't survive with her," which became one of the prevailing labels for her when she wasn't around.

But my grandfather wasn't angry. In fact, his heart grew more attached to Fatima than it did to the boy who lived for a month. This was in part due to a village magic formula that never fails: naming him after a wild animal. My grandfather named him Shibl—Lion Cub, and when he was one week old, my grandfather grew optimistic and his heart filled with joy, but the boy began to deteriorate before his parents' eyes. The wild animal name didn't protect him as the magic formula purported. It didn't ward off the Angel of Death that usually avoids going near boys with wild animal names.

It seems as though the Angel of Death is terrified by names like Asad (Lion), Shibl (Lion Cub), and Nimr (Tiger), but not names like Ahmad, Ali, and Bilal. But the magic charm was never wrong, and people continued to heed it to save their quick-to-suffer male offspring. It was never wrong except with my grandmother.

What bothered me about it was that there was no magic charm for saving girls. Humans stopped burying baby girls alive, but they didn't try to protect them with names like Shibla (Female Lion Cub) or Labwa (Lioness) or Nimra (Tigress). I don't know any girls who have such names. We don't hear about women miscarrying girls. Are there women who miscarry girls?

How come we don't hear about them? Is it because it is not a bad thing? Or because girls are destined to survive the moment they are conceived?

The magic charm didn't work, but my grandfather's prediction did come true.

He died two weeks after Fatima was born and never saw how that chunk of white flesh transformed into the most beautiful young woman in the village—into the dream that filled the mind of every young or grown man who laid eyes on her, or had her beauty described to him without even seeing her himself. He never saw if she really were like his grandmother, or more beautiful than her, or more beautiful than anything a lonely and poor widowed mother could imagine possible.

Fatima's beauty gave my grandmother "many a headache," as she says. The numerous suitors and my grandmother's efforts to keep Fatima away from them—her vanity, nervousness and the shame she felt about her mother's lowly work that would prevent her from getting a rich husband, which she believed she deserved. Matters that muddied up our life.

***

Karim works diligently while I watch the mixture become thick and stretchy, and the heat rising from it ignites the kitchen more and more. But he keeps silent, as if intentionally trying to hear something. The sound of the ladle or my movements or maybe even my breathing.

The window behind the stove is wide open. If he comes near me, I will scream at the top of my lungs. But he doesn't. He is not the wolf of the story, waiting in the dangerous forest for Little Red Riding Hood—the wolf my aunt Fatima awakened in all the men in the world—and the forest that Fatima nicknamed Beirut.

Every time I said I wanted to go to Beirut, she would make the gravity of my words apparent to me, along with the riskiness of my choice. Beirut is a forest, which she had experienced for herself when she worked at the cookie factory.

Her maternal uncle got her the job there in his capacity as foreman. My grandmother agreed to it after the women of the quarter convinced her that letting Fatima out of the house to work would help her recover from the calamity of her broken engagement. Maybe she would find a better groom. And my aunt agreed presuming her uncle would have secured a good job for her because he was in charge and "had clout" at the factory.

What that advice ended up in was hatred, not love or marriage. She hated the city and was terrified of its alleyways with all the monsters planted everywhere. That was what she wanted to convey to me.

"*Sitti* (Grandma), why didn't Little Red Riding Hood's mother go with her? Or walk her there?"

"How should I know? Maybe she was busy!"

"What work could be more important than taking care of her daughter? Especially knowing there was a wolf in the forest!!"

"Huh? *Yalla*, go to sleep. Enough of these questions. It's just a story that's supposed to happen that way!"

"Okay, but why didn't the wolf eat her there in the forest when he first saw her? Why did he wait for her to get to her grandmother's house?"

"Goodness! Will this night ever end? How should I know? Was I there with them? It's just a story that's supposed to be that way! *Yalla*, read the *Fatiha*, ask for God's protection, and go to sleep. *Aouzu bil-Laah min al-shaytan al-rajin*—I take refuge in God from the Evil One…"

I repeat after her, but I don't fall asleep until I take refuge in a convincing answer: Little Red Riding Hood must have been ugly, with kinky hair that tortured her mother whenever she combed it for her. That was why she sent her daughter to her grandmother on some errand, but she *intended* to send her into the forest without protection. Mothers might do even more horrific things to their ugly daughters.

***

A current of cold air comes streaming into the kitchen and stings my sweaty skin. I shiver and mutter a plea for God's protection from the Evil One. Karim says everything's fine now. Both air conditioners are working.

I pay him his hourly wage plus a little extra for the time he spent stirring the *mughli*.

From the kitchen window I watch him take off on his motorcycle.

The sound of the air conditioners comes to me from every direction. I shut the windows and the doors just to listen to the sound of my air conditioners, and to the reproachful tunes of Abdel Wahab, which taught me to love him.

"I remember the one who has forgotten me, and I forget the one who remembers me…"

But it isn't my favorite song because the second half of the refrain doesn't apply to me. There isn't anyone who "remembers me" or thinks about me. No man ever loved me. Not even my father. There wasn't time for me to know if he loved me, or rather, a stray hunting bullet didn't give him time to love me.

Every girl and woman I've ever known has her song. The song of her life. Except for me. I have yet to find my song.

"*A ghadan alqaak*? Will I meet you tomorrow?" might be the song of my week, but not the song of my life.

A song that would merit being my song would be about one-sided love, between two people with no shared past between them, who have never been brought together in a place or time that grants the lover the chance to express his feelings to the beloved. No doubt if it exists, it would be a very sad song. More miserable than anything a poet would think of composing.

Men have their songs, too. We know some of them from their girlfriends and wives, and I know the rest from the little window at the coffeehouse.

***

I used to spy on men at their famous sanctuary—the coffee house.

There were three coffee houses in the village. A relatively large number for the population, but the men were addicted to them, between those out of work, the lazy ones and those addicted to "*shaddeh*" —playing cards.

The coffee houses had upper rooms and high windows for air circulation. Music from the radio and television, and smoke from cheap cigarettes emanated from them.

I was small and skinny. I moved about the alleys and lanes of the village like a rat. But that was not what gave me the courage to sneak in through the small gaping hole meant to alleviate the humidity of the Mediterranean air indoors by letting in a wafts of fresh air; no, it was because I was certain no one ever noticed me, inside the coffeehouse or outside it.

I used to eavesdrop on their conversations and listen in on songs sung by Umm Kulthum, Fayzah Ahmad, and Warda, whose name they pronounced with a heavy "d" sound. But the cursing was loudest.

Smoke filled the place and collected up near the ceiling, sometimes forcing me to get out of there before I started coughing and got caught.

They did all sorts of disgusting things with abandon. They stuck their fingers in their noses and wiped the snots on the tables and chairs. They scratched their genitals openly. They farted and belched…

I didn't regret many things—not having lived with my father and grandfather—that none of my grandmother's sons survived to become my maternal uncles—or that my paternal uncle worked in Kuwait. Any man in the family could easily have been one of those coffeehouse men, sitting around playing cards with them, farting and scratching his butt, gambling, swearing ten times a minute, making light of God the way they do, as if the matter was a piece of gum they chewed randomly.

Along came a man who walked with slow steps. At his waist was a bunch of dead birds and in his hand was a long piece of paper. He wove his way between the coffeehouse patrons, telling them the names they could choose from: Jawad al-Lay—Ghadanfar—Farnaas—Balqis—Abu Zayd—Antar—Sitt Budour… Whoever wanted to play chose a name and paid a metal coin. In the end, and after all the names were bought, the man opened the last square to see the winning name: Sitt Budour!

"But last time it was Budour. That's bullshit! Budour every time…It's never Badri or Son-of-a-Bitch!!"

The losers grumble while the one who chose Sitt Budour wins the prize, which is the bunch of birds.

A primitive sort of gambling that they are hooked on, like the card games *Leekha*, *Tarneeb*, *Baloot*, and *Arbaamiyyeh*. Many of them play "the races." They bet on horses and lose while others are hooked on gambling. They head to Beirut to gamble and bet on races. I know some of their daughters from school. They don't have books or pencils or even socks.

There was the time I saw one of them cheat and pull a card out from his sleeve! I almost squealed, but another man exposed him and the whole matter ended in a humorous brawl like the brawls in Egyptian films between Ismael Yassine and Tawfik El-Deken.

People from every direction crowded in to see the battle. I came down and entered the coffee house with a number of children who had sprouted up like mushrooms. I wasn't afraid of getting hurt. I wanted to set foot on the floor of the coffee house and look up at the air circulation holes.

They kicked the children out, so we fled like rats scurrying towards the closest shelter. I rushed to my grandmother to tell her what happened. She was smiling as she listened before my aunt came from behind me and grabbed me by the ear. "What took you to the coffee house, you little trouble-maker!"

I was caught.

Ever since that day, I've never gone near the coffee house again because I believed my aunt would tell the women, and they would tell their husbands, who might run into me and give me a beating.

***

When I nearly choke on my tears during my nights of despair, I go out onto the balcony that used to be the dangerous *tercina*. I sit facing the sea, dreaming I might one day touch those boat-and ship-lanterns reflecting on the water, wishing I hadn't survived my birth or the time I fell from here.

But Umm Najib's prediction came true. Girls kick death in the butt.

Umm Najib herself hurled the ball of death from her own goal to that of her robust husband who never complained of an ailment a day in his life, not even a headache.

She was fighting to hold on in her deathbed while he was out shopping for household needs and telling everyone who asked hopelessly about his wife, "It's in God's hands."

The next morning the sheikh from the mosque announced he was dead.

The people in the village thought the sheikh was mistaken and he had intended to say Umm Najib, not her husband. But it was him.

He died in perfect health and tranquility.

At his funeral, I envied him because he didn't suffer. He died happy.

The women mourners sang lamentations and said death had double-crossed him. But that didn't bother me. Death was permitted to double-cross us because it didn't leave us the opportunity to rebuke or place blame or even to regret.

After his death, Umm Najib stopped mentioning his evil deeds—from his beating her to his marrying a woman from Aleppo he met when he was selling textiles in Syria.

When mentioning him, she no longer repeated her favorite saying, "Why would I want to remember you, you quince. I choke on every bite." Bou Najib had been the quince. Hard and dry and gets stuck in your throat. But then he became a piece of *halqoun*—Turkish delight. She started referring to him as "the late Bou Najib, God rest his soul." She would say it with sorrow and a pang of guilt because she was the one who had brought Azrael into their home where he went to the wrong bed.

***

My grandmother regained her health a little bit that morning, reviving my hope what had happened to her was just a momentary setback.

I fed her, bathed her, and dressed her in clean clothes. She fell asleep, so I took advantage of the opportunity to enjoy a short nap.

But I woke from a terrifying dream in which I saw the clock strike twelve. The strokes came with frightening heartbeats—as if my dream signified the hour of her death.

I looked at the nearest clock—it was ten o'clock.

I looked at my grandmother, holding my finger below her nostrils. She was breathing.

I got up to make myself a cup of anise tea, hoping it would calm me down. But it didn't help.

I sat watching over her, counting her breaths, and I took her pulse.

It was 12:01, then 12:02, then 12:10.

Her pulse was warm and vigorous.

I breathed a sigh of relief and put the nightmare out of my mind. But it didn't grant me much time. I lived it twelve hours later.

How did the clock hands deceive me? How did I overlook the fact that the day has more than one 12 o'clock?!!!

12 noon and 12 midnight.

***

I moisten a cotton ball with *mazaher*—orange blossom water—and wipe my face. Then I rub it over the veins of my wrists. I have been doing that for ages to calm my fears. I am not sure who I learned this method from, or whether I learned it or made it up. But I remember a cosmetology expert talking on television one time recommending spraying perfume on the veins because this made it intermingle well with the body and made the fragrance last longer.

Mazaher doesn't last longer if it touches the veins. Rather, it lodges in the soul. For ages we have believed that it brings back the soul. Not by some magic action, but because it is a soul itself.

The soul of bitter orange blossoms.

Its distinguishing characteristic is that it is so sweet and potent a soul, it has the power to revive the unconscious and bring it back to life.

Have you ever seen how a soul transforms into water? It is not a miracle or a fantasy, but something scientific. A soul is more like vapor in the human imagination and, when vapor in its turn crashes into something cold, it transforms into liquid. A crash like that has to take place in order to trigger such an extraordinary action. And even though it is not a rare occurrence, only a few know of it or take interest in it because people are terrified of souls and death.

No doubt you have read that novel *Perfume* which was so startling to me and kept me lying awake in my bed at night scared to death of that demented criminal.

I didn't find it in your library but rather loaned it from a university student who used to pass by the co-op every week. The title caught my attention, so I asked her about the novel. She seemed highly enthusiastic towards my question, as though she were about to domesticate an ignorant village girl and usher her into the world of enlightenment and culture. She lent me the novel and said she would come back the following week to pick it up. She hoped I would finish it in a week. I didn't tell her I finished it in two consecutive nights because eliciting her excitement again wasn't something I was prepared for. I was in a tremendous state of shock that had thrown me off balance for several days.

A madman searching for that secret goes around melting things to release their vapor. And the vapor transforms into drops which are its clear, distilled, undiluted and pure essence. My grandmother didn't know any character from any novel. And she wouldn't have believed this one's story despite it not being any stranger than her own stories about ghouls and *jinns*. And she wouldn't have known how to pronounce the name Süskind, even if she were to join him in distilling the soul of bitter orange blossoms in order to extract what they call '*mazaher,*' most of which she sold for a meager profit that made her happy.

I used to help her pick the orange blossoms.

We would go to every orange tree of the "*Bousfeir*" type though I like the term "*Narenj*"—Bitter Orange—as it is referred to in books. It is the only type that is useful for this industry of ours, which is a good thing for the tree. After all, the fact its fruit is bitter and inedible makes it a threat to its own survival. That is why it revealed itself to human beings and gave them the idea that it would be good to distill its soul, so they wouldn't chop it down and make it extinct in its struggle for survival. That's what Darwin taught me in your library and of which I found numerous explanations while loitering there.

The bitter orange tree fought for its survival and continued existence by being useful in the production of *mazaher*. We would go to every stray tree where the owners didn't mind having its blossoms plucked. We would ask permission sometimes and pluck every last flower, one batch after another, week after week. We would gather them and then go to other villages, especially the coastal ones, where the citrus groves had thrived, before their inhabitants abandoned them, and all their earthly bounty died.

***

I wash the fruit.

The loquats and mulberries ripened early.

I bought them at Monoprix! I didn't feel at home there despite the long hours I spent between the aisles of canned goods, cooking oils, confectionary goods, paper napkins and cleaning solutions. That Monoprix was a scary entity that made me aware of my own insignificance and bewilderment. I asked myself while browsing all sorts of goods I never imagined existed, "What was it that brought me here?"

The situation was much like the melancholy of the first days of a new school year. I always cried on the first day. That was not limited to just the first years but right up to my last year. It was the year I didn't finish, when I discovered your library was enough for me, and the best teacher at the school hadn't read half of one of your smallest books.

What was it that brought me to Beirut? It is such an arid place. The air is too heavy for my lungs to bear. When I walk down the street, I never come across a single tree that might provide me with some shade. I see buildings that have been eaten by dust and pollution and shacks made of zinc sheets teeming with children who resemble the beggars of Sidon and Khalde highway.

I used to see them every workday. They would congregate at bus stops and hound everyone with chewing gum and cigarette lighters, or with empty hands. They were the overture to my arduous daily trip and the prelude to the worst of the stops that needed to be made: crossing the highway.

I would stand there defeated watching all the passing vehicles of various shapes and sizes. Defeated before entering the battle.

How shall I cross? When? And what do the people inside the vehicles say when they see my hesitation, my shame and my desperate glances? Whenever I see people crossing the highway, I search for those strange facial features that show their fear of death and their adherence to life. This is despite its constant humiliation of them, where they look like farm roosters that the poultryman has grabbed in preparation for butchering but decides to set free, granting them a few more days of life because there isn't enough demand from customers today.

Numerous images crowd my head as I cross the highway—images summarizing my life in black and white. Those terrifying moments spent crossing the highway were the "negatives" of my life which I have so often considered to be a long life, despite it's being no more than three decades!

Many people have died here. Trucks have sent them flying dozens and hundreds of meters, in all directions. That's why I don't try to guess in which direction the car or truck will throw me as it ends a life about which I no longer like anything, not even my grandmother's stories or a loaf of bread I eat hot off the *Saj* oven, or the huge buildings scattered along the two sides of the highway.

I had fallen in love with those buildings at first sight. Some had marble facades, others glass and yet others, aluminum. They were all sorts of colors and had balconies of different shapes. I could never get my fill of looking at them.

Later on, when I got a job at the co-op, and the trip from Khalde became mandatory, I had enough time to memorize every single one of them and to choose the most beautiful one with utmost care. I often wondered how fate might turn its course and allow me to go inside one of those buildings. It might be possible were one of my sisters to marry a man of means who would bring her to live in an apartment in Khalde! I never imagined myself as the bride. No one ever expected me to get married or thought I had any thoughts of doing so. This was true even during the days when I badgered my grandmother and had heated arguments with her, demanding she give me the money to buy a gold pound with a gold chain. She had no idea I wanted the money so I could catch the attention of a suitor who might go after my money, as many young women looking to marry were accused of doing.

The day she fell and became bedridden was memorable. I asked for assistance from her younger sister, who refused, citing the need to look after her children as an excuse. My grandmother, who wasn't deceived by this lie, said, "She's busy with her children? Hah! She thinks she managed to get married because of her intelligence and her beauty! If it hadn't been for the stack of six gold bracelets on her wrist, who would have let that dandy's son marry her? I'm the one who told her to buy gold. I wanted her to keep track of herself and not end up a spinster like her aunt. She had a big butt like her, too. Now she doesn't want to take care of me even though I was the one who took care of her when I used my savings from "*al-sa'ey*" (watering)—and took her to Sidon to buy her the six-bracelet set."

My grandmother would repeat the story of "*al-sa'ey*" as if it happened yesterday, not five decades ago. Her aunt's husband used to bring big rolls of brown paper and glue from Beirut which the girls of the quarter would use to make paper sacks of different sizes, and he would pay them wages according to the weight of their output. They would "water" the paper with the glue, and that's where the name came from.

The girls would wait for him at the top of the street, worried he would give the materials to some other girls.

For the price of "*al-sa'ey*" she bought gold for her poor daughters, and thus the jingling of gold bracelets entered our quarter, as my grandmother would say, for there was no meaning to buying gold if a woman didn't shake her hand and let everyone hear it jingle. That was the sound that delighted the "dandy's son" and made him covet the six bracelets—and maybe there were more? Maybe he was willing to get himself entangled in a marriage contract just a few months before that limited-time supply got cut off when paper sack factories arrived on the scene?

Like my grandmother who had been saving for years, I saved up for three years, but not to buy a ring. I couldn't guess how much it was, but I wanted it.

I started picking fights with her every day so I could buy a gold pound with a gold chain.

"All the girls are wearing gold except me because I'm fatherless and no one even looks at me. Your whole life you've put me to work and made me carry things for you. Then you mock me with a few coins even a beggar wouldn't accept."

Finally, my grandmother conceded. Throwing the money into my lap, she said, "Here, take it and get off my back. I was saving it for my final days."

It wasn't till I wore the gold pound necklace that I felt regret. It was like a noose around my neck. And so, I put it back into its velvety box and asked my grandmother to hide it away.

I didn't open the velvety box again until a week ago when I sold it.

My sweet grandmother would have permitted me to do so for the sake of a rare day like this. She would have given me all her savings to make my lifelong dream come true.

***

I taste the loquats but don't find their promised sweetness. Not because they ripened before their time, but because the taste of things in my mouth here had changed.

The dust-and smoke-laden air filled my mouth, saliva and stomach.

Even if I were to bring the prickly orange pears from our own tree here, they wouldn't have the same flavor they have out on the balcony facing the sea.

Whenever inexperienced visitors from cities come to visit us, they sing the praises of our fruits and debate over how best to describe their flavor. They don't know the reason for such exceptional sweetness. Nor do they recognize the fresh air that got mixed into the juice or the clean rainwater that the fruits drank up all through the winter.

We laugh after they've gone, saying, "What a bunch of idiots those Beirutis are!!! Dumbbells! That's God's gift to them…"

We would accuse them of stupidity, just as they accused us of the same. Does anyone win this silly game?

If only we had met one day between the ends of summer and the beginnings of autumn. I would have taken you to the cactus tree and picked its fruit in front of you using "the stem" tool with its long stick. My grandmother made it to avoid that fruit's prickly thorns when picking it. And I would have previously extracted the core from beneath the rough skin which is always covered with those prickly thorns and offered it to you so you don't feel the slightest twinge.

During the picking of harmful weeds or the picking of olives, prickly pears or jujube fruits, the tiny thorns tortured our skin equally, and we used to endure them as though they were part of our skin.

And that is how my love for you was. Thorns residing in my body. I endured them because they were the means of getting to the honeycomb of the fruit.

I chose pomegranate because the fruits of that tree used to guard the door to your room during my attempts to sneak in. I used to see their shadow despite the window's opaqueness. How could those studded crowns be concealed?

I was telling you—while I imagined you being there with me in the room—that a spell was cast on a queen one time, transforming her into a pomegranate tree. That would make the pomegranate blossom a princess! And its bewildering color, somewhere between purple and the red of sunset, was the most exemplary for virgin princesses.

I used to collect pomegranate crowns and save them until they wilted completely. But whoever called the pomegranate the queen of fruit must never have seen a pineapple. How could the Ancient Greeks have known about it before the explorer ships brought home that tropical fruit?

I was roaming through the fields stretched out before me. I admit that I love them despite their cruelty and aware too that the soil that sprouted all this vegetation held within it so many people's bones and stories that don't die out quickly because they are stronger than glass and mirrors—corpses buried during that span of time immediately following a horrifying epidemic. My grandmother passed down the story from her great grandfather about how the burials lasted days because the few survivors were not able to bury so many dead, and the calamity and the fear of contracting the disease themselves confounded their strong bodies which had been built stone by stone with a kind of cement called bulgur wheat. It was a story entrusted from one ancestor to another, generation to generation.

It was a coincidence I was born in this spot of the vast universe where everything which elates the soul arouses suspicion. Where the days of frost are longer than the few moments of warmth, and the months of summer heat and drought are longer than the fleeting moments of autumn. Where every female—who never chose to be born female—has to justify her arrival into the world and her survival in it—and her laughter if ever it's too loud, or her gasps, if ever they burst out…to justify her salvation from sickness and death, and her insistence on clinging to life, despite her not gaining anything from it except its vengeance and whatever burnt remnants get stuck to the bottom of the pot.

My grandmother's brother-in-law used to lecture the neighborhood girls and threaten them maliciously. "You can tell from the way a girl walks if she's done something." Then at a subsequent session he would repeat the idea with a more alarming tone, "You can tell from the way she walks if she's a girl or a woman."

After hearing such statements, girls who were sitting down hated to stand up to head home. They would get up grudgingly and walk, barely able to move, stumbling all over the place, as if every last one of them had forgotten how to walk. They lost a lot of their pureness of heart on the journey to maturity. They were forced to prove their chastity and to remind everyone of it even when the occasion didn't call for it.

Now I forgive them for being proud of the blood of their hymen on the "sheets" of their marital bed. Putting that intimate blood on display was most certainly a heavy burden, but it coincided with trills of jubilation and the serving of cold drinks and congratulations.

I will prepare the pomegranate juice tomorrow with some bubbly water and oranges. Your glass will look enticing when I leave a sprig of mint floating on its surface, just as the page of your aborted meeting with Fatima floats on the surface of my pain and suffering.

3

Night falls heavily on the city. It sounds like a belching monster as it crashes against the buildings.

Here I am not on that balcony, which is on the brink of collapse. I am not looking out at the sea stretched before me and the coastal village that separates me from it. The house I know nothing but that Mary and her daughter abandoned during the "War of the Mountain," which they never came back to except as two Australian tourists.

The valley is not here below the balcony now, beckoning me to relive the experience of falling, so I might understand exactly what happened that day, which kept coming back to me in my recurring nightmares with obscure and painful scenes.

During the first years, there was something within me that refused to sleep when it sensed that same nightmare approaching.

That recurred for a time. Then I started being afraid of insomnia, and I preferred the nightmare because I knew it and had learned its pain by heart. I also knew where it began and ended, and that inevitably it would end. As for that excruciating sleeplessness, its pain did not even have the beginning of an end.

My misery and physical exhaustion intensified, and I started sleeping like the cold corpse of a dead jackal. Sometimes, even at its terrifying highpoints, the nightmare was unable to wake me up. It would devour me to the last bite and last drop of blood without the least bit of resistance from me.

The windows of the facing building have closed curtains. The yellow of their thick fabric is pale from the dust, the sun and rain. What is behind those curtains? Women cooking and cleaning the whole day long and braying like donkeys at night from their swollen feet and aching backs?

Do city women suffer in pain like us?

Quite unexpectedly, a slender woman wearing a scanty white top steps outside. I take a careful look to determine if I am really seeing what I am seeing or imagining it. She's in nothing but a t-shirt, and this becomes obvious when she raises her hand to take another puff from her cigarette, which is slender like her.

The woman tosses the cigarette butt and heads into the room, but she stops suddenly with her back still turned to the balcony to lift her arms and take off the t-shirt.

The spoon drops from my hand and I gasp while my heart races. Has she gone crazy? Or are we in a movie theater?

Her body turns into a shadow, and she disappears into the room. Then the lights go out.

The shock has frozen me in place and paralyzed my thoughts.

Was what I saw real?

For whom was this woman doing her strip tease? A particular person or just whoever was watching? Or me?

Saada's message becomes a refuge. I escape to anything that will make me forget what I saw.

What was Aisha thinking about now? Did she really ask for me? Or was it a ploy from Saada to get me to pay the hospital bill?

I heave a deep sigh. Yes, that's what was going on. They were baiting me to pay, since I was the only one of Aisha's daughters employed; somehow their husbands always knew every piastre I got paid, though I could never figure out how.

I wouldn't go. Let them figure out for themselves what to do. If they had Aisha discharged from the hospital and postponed the operation, then they would bear the responsibility for her death if she died.

But, what about me? Wouldn't I be responsible? Wouldn't I be a murderer?

Let these thoughts leave me. I'm just a girl cooking for a man she loves and never loved any other.

I sold the harvest of my entire lifetime and my grandmother's lifetime for the sake of this banquet, and I'm not going to abandon it now.

***

I pour the *mughli* into clear serving bowls and soak the almonds, pine nuts and walnuts in water to use for garnish tomorrow.

Is it true what I am thinking about right now? That you are coming here to eat what I have cooked for you? Will you shake my hand and examine my scar the way you did on your engagement day twenty-five years ago?

That night, the owl returned to the carob tree as was its habit every spring. Everyone had been expecting it to come, but it frightened my aunt.

She slapped her chest and gasped. Then she shut the door to the balcony and shut the window so she wouldn't hear the ill-omened hooting.

That day might have gotten folded up inside the notebook of oblivion had my aunt not brought it up a few months later. It was part of her grudging commentary on the broken engagement when she reminded everyone that her intuition had been right: "I knew it wasn't going to end well…because the owl hooted the night of the engagement."

"What's 'Bull!' got to do with 'Hello'?" Tahani chided. Fatima grimaced, so Tahani tried to make amends. "I mean, this is fate. It's God's will. What's the owl got to do with it?"

Tahani didn't try to hide her joy over my aunt's break-up because that was beyond her ability. Her hopes of catching the attention of the *Hakim* and his family didn't go up, but his not being engaged to Fatima anymore did give her a lot of gratification.

My aunt placed much of the blame for her bad luck on the owl.

On hot spring nights, she forced us to close the balcony door and window, so she wouldn't hear the owl hooting. My grandmother and I did not have the courage to contradict her. We would rather drip with sweat than argue with her. But our nights were easier than hers. My grandmother would finish her story and fall asleep. Then I would switch to another story and fall asleep in the middle of it in peace, not even noticing the heat. My aunt on the other hand spent the night awake. She didn't make a sound, didn't cry, or grieve as she had done after her fiancé left her, but she tossed and turned a lot. The rustling of her hair entered my dreams, where I would borrow it for myself. I would dream it was my hair, and it was flying in the breeze as I swung on the branch of a flowering almond tree while you pushed me.

I feel guilty towards my aunt. I pray she will marry the richest and handsomest man in the world and be happy.

I wish I could tell her that the owl is innocent and not to blame, for it had appeared during the days of the engagement and had been a good omen. As for the day when the *Hakim's* aunt came to utter those few words, "*Ma fi naseeb*—Wasn't meant to be," there was no owl. In fact, it was summer, very hot, and the trees were deserted.

Both of my hands and all ten of my fingers were immersed in the ripe tomatoes floating in a huge pot. Twenty skinny girls like me could fit around it in a circle. And my grandmother stood in front of a cardboard box of tomatoes with a knife in her hand, cutting away the bruised parts. It was the end of the season—the time when she would get boxes of ripe and half over-ripe tomatoes from the nearby coastal farmers for a quarter of their price and sometimes for free.

She got the fire ready and asked me why the rest of the children were late.

"They're coming," I said calmly.

We children loved juicing the tomatoes. It was more like playing than working. We'd squish them between our fingers and out came their juice and their seeds. We'd "splash" each other and challenge each other over whose elbows the red sauce would reach first.

Some of the neighborhood children had come; I didn't have a single friend among them. They only came to compete in such games. Then a woman came. I had never seen her before, but my grandmother was taken aback when she saw her. The woman was frowning. She came in and stepped aside with my grandmother and my aunt. I didn't catch but one phrase, which she kept repeating, "Wasn't meant to be."

Our house became like a big pot of tomato sauce, boiling over with red bubbles of another sort. My grandmother and aunt's breaths became like the steam coming out from the bubbles, burning themselves with it before everyone else.

My grandmother refused to tell me the story of the ghoul's daughter. Choked up with tears, she said, "*Yalla*. Go to sleep." I didn't really grasp the disaster that had stricken the family until later, when I saw my aunt—that beautiful creature—change into a grim and violent one, as though the mere fact of a man leaving her was the end of the world!

Why should I disapprove? A girl like her will have left school after getting engaged and no longer cared about anything except her trousseau—a collection of delicate personal and household items she would take with her into her new life as a married woman. She even traveled to Damascus to buy some of it, and spent hours hunched over her crochet hook making all sorts of things. A girl who had all that beauty and pride, and all those envious girls and the rejected suitors and broken hearts. It was only logical for her to break; or rather, to topple over.

My ears caught wind of a lot of nasty gossiping.

"The *Hakim* left Fatima and skedaddled. Maybe he saw her doing something! No, he got married abroad. No, she's an elementary school dropout and he's a doctor. He's a fool. She can find someone better than him, the poor thing. He broke her heart and her spirit. Where's he going to find someone more beautiful than her. Hey, foreign girls are pretty, but the beauty here is natural and lasting, doesn't wear out right away. I mean, he waited to travel out of the country to leave her. Something definitely had to happen between them. Maybe she gave herself to him, and he hated her afterwards for being too easy."

There was a lot of evil in people's souls. The kind of evil that was even heavier than the souls themselves. And I hated how she bore it.

But my aunt got better one day when she reached a final decision: her mother should quit washing bedsheets for the nursing home and quit harvesting bunches of parsley and purslane. We lived through months of my aunt's bickering with my grandmother and nagging her to quit her lowly work. It had gotten stuck in my aunt's mind during her long hours of seclusion that this was the reason her fiancé had run off. My grandmother finally agreed to it under one condition. "Find yourself a job first and secure yourself in it, and then I'll quit this work of mine which you don't approve of."

My aunt Fatima worked just a few months at the cookie factory—where her maternal uncle was the foreman—and she used to bring home packages of the "cream-filled" cookies I loved, unlike her. She would always—for some strange reason—scrape off the cream from between the two layers and throw it away before eating the plain cookies.

After a short period of performing that grueling shift, she skipped going to work three days in a row. The time for her to get up would come, but she would just stay asleep. I assumed she was on vacation, but when her uncle came by to scold her, she told him she was never going back to that job. She offered some flimsy excuses. "The stink of the rancid cream bothers me. The girls are nasty to me. The long trip is tiring. The Ouzaai area is crowded. My pay barely covers the cost of transportation."

But she alluded to another reason during one of her conversations with Tahani. "I want to work in a shop with clean and important people, not a bunch of laborers and people in dire circumstances who desire me and make my life miserable. I mean, why on earth would I accept any one of them? Don't they ask themselves this question? What do they have I could possibly want from them?"

To put it another way, she discovered the best person at that factory was her uncle, and she knew well the poverty under which his family was sinking.

Tahani used to chime in with Fatima and tell the same kinds of stories about rejecting suitors—mostly from her own imagination—and about her desire to be engaged to a man who could pull her out of poverty. But Tahani's strong tone turned out to be shaky, which became evident later when she married the first passerby who mistakenly came knocking at her parents' door.

They would prattle back and forth, gazing at the sea and snacking on pumpkin seeds like a couple of parrots. Then one would ask the other, "Shall we go to Sidon like you mentioned?" They'd agree on a time to go shopping, to buy new clothes and also to put all accusations of poverty to rest.

My grandmother used to give things to my aunt without question. She'd "cut a chunk of her own flesh to feed her" if only she would be satisfied with her life and be healed of her first humiliating defeat. But nothing healed my aunt. The fire stayed in its place and, to this day, she continued asking herself the same question, "Why did he leave me?"

The women would say—whenever my aunt was not around—that he was staying with his friends in Beirut when he would come for vacations. When they saw his Russian wife, they bit their lips, and their eyes popped out. This was because her hair was brown, not blond like most of the Russian women the young men of the village brought back with them when they returned from their fruitful university studies!

Talking about him in front of my aunt was forbidden, and the women knew their limits with her. Wounding her pride turned her from a kitten into a tiger on the prowl, and when she got angry, she aimed her bullets straight at the heart. Harsh words and direct shots at their flaws. But they weren't only afraid of her, they also felt pity and considered her a wronged woman. "A luckless beauty."

Those few months in Beirut made her imagine the city as a forest, amidst people who were not pleased in the least by her thick village accent or her loud voice—which was considered normal in the village. In the eyes of the factory workers, she was a beautiful but naïve girl, and she was the object of ridicule from those girls who envied her beauty, good health, rosy complexion, perfect teeth and hair. One of those girls made fun of a random word she said, and when I heard the way my aunt tensed up while telling the story of what happened, I swore never to say that word outside the house. Until this day, I avoid saying "*dabwa*" and make sure to use words like "purse" or "wallet" instead.

On the way to work, she was subjected to all sorts of harassment making her hate that trip. It was also because of the way people stared at her on the bus, where passengers were seated facing each other, she preferred to take a "service" taxi even though it was more expensive. Her salary was no longer worth the suffering she had to bear, so for that and other reasons, she decided to quit working and stay home.

My grandmother didn't leave the nursing home by choice. It was shut down due to the war, and the residents were moved to locations far away from the war zone. This was something I had no understanding of except that it was called the "War of the Mountain." It appeared we Muslims had been expelled, so we forced the Christians out—because they had corroborated with Israel—and we pillaged their homes, including Mary's house!!

When my grandmother found out that Mary's house had been robbed, she pounded her chest in despair and wailed openly, not fearing the armed men or the slanderers. The meager income that she referred to as "a little rock propping up a huge clay urn" had been cut off. The "rock" was gone so the urn toppled over, and to stop it from breaking, my grandmother carried it on her back and went on bearing its weight until it crushed her bones.

To compensate, she increased her work in the fields and in farming and olive oil soap production. All of this had a bearing on me, too, in my capacity as her captive—not free-willed—assistant. It was before I resigned from that tiring occupation and turned my back on my grandmother at night, just as Fatima used to do, and chose to sleep in another room.

Suddenly, my aunt Fatima comes crashing into the place. Everywhere I look, I see and hear her crying those bitter tears she cried the night of her break-up. She's blowing her nose and sobbing under the covers, raving with delirium from the fever that consumed her beautiful body.

I see her grabbing me by the ear and shoving me against the wall, threatening to shear my scalp—more hideously than her sister had done—because she found out that I had been visiting your mother. And to break both my legs for having stepped foot inside your house.

Whenever I slipped your diary or any pictures of you under my pillow, or stole a sniff or quick feel of them, my heart would start pounding as I looked over at my aunt's bed and imagined her discovering what I had. What if she discovered that the dagger that pierced her heart was right there under a pillow only three steps away?

Throughout those nights, I thought of girls like me who had fallen in love and were still in love with their maternal or paternal aunt's fiancé. We were all inside the circle of suspicion. In my head, I rattled off the girls' names of our quarter and the neighboring quarters. I don't despise them; I sympathize with them. It comforts me to believe there are girls aching from all that pain and overpowered by all that regret. It's not fair for anyone to blame me, for we are all guilty.

What if she were to show up now unexpectedly and find out I have invited you here and have loved you since my first years of life? In other words, for as long as she has loved you? And that not only did I share with her the tragedies of being fatherless, forlorn, and lonely, but of loving one man, too?

I see her in the white coconut powder, which resembles her chest and her thighs and every hidden part of her body even the sun doesn't see. She's also in the scent of rose water she always sprinkled on her body after a bath, and in the beads of *moghrabieh* couscous that my grandmother was hurrying to roll into little balls for you before being surprised by your sudden departure. Won't it make her feel better that tomorrow you will eat the *moghrabieh* she had promised you before you left?

No, nothing will make her feel better. The feeling the people closest to her were betraying her—and how horribly had he betrayed her—would resurrect all the wounds out of their graves, including my grand-mother's wounds.

My grandmother continued to hope she might see you, if only in her dreams, so she could ask you the reason you left her daughter. In fact, one time she rushed to see Umm Najib to tell her about a dream. "Last night I dreamt something good—God bless the Prophet. The *Hakim* came up to me in the street and said, 'I was sick, and I was afraid to get married'" Umm Najib interrupts her and says, "Sand cannot be kneaded into dough, and what is broken cannot be fixed. Get up and stop telling me dreams about this and that."

Umm Najib didn't give my grandmother the slightest glimmer of hope. That was the opposite of what everyone was used to getting from Umm Najib as she had an insatiable appetite for interpreting our dreams. In fact, Umm Najib used to dream about us, too.

Umm Najib smooths out her scarf under her white hair. I can hear the dry cracks in her fingers scraping against the soft scarf. She says in complete seriousness, "I saw you in a dream, Amal. You were wearing green with green and carrying a green purse! Do you know what that means? Your husband is going to come into a fortune." Amal believes her. Her smile twitches, and she rushes home to give the good news to her bankrupt husband.

"Listen, Sabah. I saw in a dream you had a hen sitting on two eggs. One hatched and the other one didn't. It means you are going to get pregnant with twins and give birth to only one of them."

She dreamed about everyone except me.

She never called to me to interpret a dream or predict anything about me. Was I too difficult for her? Or was she not expecting me to have dreams like everyone else who lived in the quarter? Why didn't she see me in a dream wearing a violet dress? Because that wasn't a familiar color in our neighborhood? And because violets didn't grow in our soil? She might have said, "mulberry" or "eggplant," but she never singled me out in those visions of hers.

I go into the bedroom, take out the mulberry dress, then put it back in its place. Mulberry, not blue. So, will you like it? Did I make a bad choice?

The truth is, if love can be considered a choice, I made a bad one choosing you.

In fact, it's a betrayal. What I am doing is a betrayal, something despicable.

I am going to call you and cancel our appointment. I'll make up any excuse. What do you and I have to do with each other after all these years? What will change if you see me or not? If you taste my cooking or not? I must be cured of you, must forget you and go on with my life, which I have deprived myself of living.

I will go to the hospital and see Aisha in her weak condition. Perhaps I will get an apology from her. Maybe she will say, "Forgive me," and my eyes will well up with tears. Or it's possible I will pay the bill without even going into Aisha's room, preferring to wait to hear the outcome of the surgery from the alleyways of Sidon where I had gotten addicted to roaming around browsing the shop windows.

I write a text message.

Hello. I hope you are well.

My apologies but due to an emergency we will have to cancel our date for tomorrow.

All that is left to do is hit "send." Will my finger obey me?

***

In the closet, where the mulberry of the dress rains down tirelessly, I come across the white satin pajama set. It is much more beautiful than anything I have seen in our village's wedding trousseaus.

I wanted something angelic to sleep in during the night of our meeting—to celebrate the event, so I could wear something to make me suitable for the dream about to come true. I bought a sexy one too:

lace and satin, short pants with two slits on the sides, the top with thin straps and soft lace that delicately hugs the breasts. I bought it from Beirut, not from our village shop, so no one would suspect anything. The prettiest one in the village shop wasn't half as pretty as this one, either, and I chose Beirut because it was not the place where my acquaintances shopped, so no one would know my secret.

This is what I wanted to sleep in the night of your arrival. I didn't want it to touch me before you had greeted me with a handshake.

I put on the pajama set quickly as though someone is going to enter and catch me naked. I put it on and throw myself onto the bed. I pick up my diary and read some of the last things I wrote. Then I think about where I should place it, so you'll stumble onto it by a fabricated coincidence!

I fall asleep.

The bird flees from my hand, and its soft feathers fly about in all directions. I tumble towards the brook. Here, there are hundreds of skulls of ancestors who died of cholera. I sprout baby bird feathers. I'm alarmed because horrible smells are emanating from me. The smells will expose me in front of everyone. People will know what I'm hiding under my clothes. I dream that the soil will conceal me forever, and the dreams intertwine with the nightmares while a woman wails in lament over her child…

I wake from my sleep.

I didn't send the message.

Ah! The mobile is in the kitchen!

I return to my sleep and postpone sending the message until morning. I will let my dreams guide me to what I should do.

The bird flees from my hand and its feathers fly about in all directions. I tumble towards the valley and sway with the wind towards the carob tree. The sound of a sad and bereaved mother's ululation echoes in the valley. I don't understand a word of what she is saying, but I know it is about a mother who lost her baby.

I look up to the sky and see God smiling at me. He will not throw me into hell and will not burn me because my skin is very delicate, and my tummy is small and can't tolerate the cups of Zaqqum. God loves me and will not kill me now…God loves me. I grab hold of the carob tree branches and scream.

Ahhhhh!

***

Something was hurting me, but I couldn't pinpoint it. Everything in me was hurting, but I survived.

Maybe this was heaven I had been transported to.

Everything around me was quiet. There was a scent of light perfume mixed with something that smelled like alcohol or from a pharmacy. Then something moved in front of me—a human shadow. I could almost hear him exhaling. He came closer and asked me questions.

I heard him but was unable to reply.

"What's your name?"

"How old are you?"

"How many do you see?"

I glimpse the shadow of a hand but not any fingers. Concentrating on it wears me out, so I shut my eyes again. And in the darkness, I clearly hear the Kurdish woman singing to her lost baby.

He was an infant, and she hadn't found anyone to look after him while she worked at "Bou Saleh Greenhouses," where she picked radishes and parsley and strawberries. She put him down at the end of the row and walked away. It seems that when she got as far as the strawberry patch, she craved a strawberry. She looked all around to make sure no one was looking and just before she bit into the strawberry, she felt her breasts stiffen. They were filling up with milk, which meant it was time to nurse her baby. He hadn't started crying to be fed as he usually did. She dropped the basket for collecting the radishes and parsley and ran off. Everything was scattered except the strawberry she forgot between her two fingers. She didn't find her baby. She sprinkled dirt over her body, screamed and then she ran all over the place searching for the sound of his crying, which she didn't hear anywhere.

She was found unconscious, bloodied with strawberries. Abou Saleh gave her some time off to look for her child, but she never came back to work. She continued searching for him, even looking for him at the gypsies' camps. She accused them of stealing him, but even the police didn't believe her.

She returned to stay with her relatives who lived in the annex connected to my grandmother's house. When night fell, she would sing a lullaby for her baby and never stopped wiping her tears, which I could tell from her voice behind the wall separating us. She sang for him to fall asleep in warmth and safety and didn't quieten down until her voice was drained to its very end.

I remember the tune, but I don't remember the words because they were in Kurdish. And that wasn't bothersome or distressing because I didn't search for a translation. I felt certain I understood the soul of that lullaby: heartbreaking loss.

The only thing I regretted was I never did recall that lullaby. It was one of the things that I lost forever.

***

I look up at the ceiling where there are no cracks—unlike the ones at my grandmother's house I could imagine however I want.

I try to go back to sleep with the lullaby resounding in my head while straining to imagine what those words might be.

Whatever happened to that woman and her infant? I was six years older than him, and logic says, despite the passing of so much time, I will always be six years older than him, so now he must be a twenty-four-year-old young man.

I used to catch myself looking firmly into the faces of young men I estimated to be around his age. I would search for that lullaby in their features, for the mother's voice and her longing for her infant and her fear of his dying of hunger.

I used to wish I would find him, so I could hold his hand and take him to the strawberry field where his mother, who had most likely died by now, had lost him.

She disappeared suddenly, but her song didn't. Maybe it diminished slightly as though it had moved a few steps away. Her relatives also disappeared. They paid the final rent and said they were going back to al-Hasaka in Syria. I don't remember anything about them—as if they had been a mirage. And whenever I ask the neighborhood folks about them and about that Kurdish woman's lullaby, they act like they don't know anything about it and fall silent for an instant that seems an eternity. They just stare at me, and charge me with the accusation that has haunted me: madness!

The madness they mean isn't the loss of wits, but the imagining of things that have no basis in reality—inventing people no womb ever gave birth to—imagining songs no tongue ever composed.

Even my grandmother claimed she didn't remember—that it had happened long ago, even before I was born. "You might not have been born yet."

The word 'might' was what confirmed my statement and invalidated theirs. Yes, I had. I had been born and had made it past my first years of childhood, and I used to cry while the Kurdish woman sang. My grandmother asked me to forget the matter because tragedies fall on the heads of those who remember them.

This explained the tragedies that struck everyone who had lived in that annex:

The martyrdom of Umm Hassan the Palestinian woman's son; the fleeing of Abbas's daughter with the Israeli soldiers; the suicide of Karima's husband with a gulp of insecticide ...

***

We received news about everyone who had ever lived in the annex except the Kurdish woman.

Karima got married to her late husband's brother and lived with the second wife as her servant.

Abbas's son joined the army and built a house for the family. He married a beautiful woman despite his own ugliness. It wasn't unheard of for army employees and policemen to get the most beautiful wives since they were early risers and chose the best available, the choicest fruit from the top of the box. On the other hand, school teachers, for example, woke up just after them, and so they would get "the leftovers" as Umm Najib described the situation.

Umm Hassan died at Al-Bass refugee camp in Sidon. Hassan's clothes were buried with her in accordance with her final wishes.

His *fedayeen* clothes, especially, were something I don't forget. I'd never seen him in anything else. I was even convinced that he slept in them because I once saw him asleep wearing his *fedayeen* pants with his weapon over his waist, that was all. I used to invite Umm Hassan to have coffee with my grandmother after the dawn call to prayer. It wasn't his weapon or his clothes or his bulging muscles that frightened me, but his dark complexion.

He was very dark-skinned. I didn't know any other family besides Umm Hassan's with such dark skin.

The girls were dark, too. I would laugh at myself when I recalled how I used to compare them to eggplant, especially because their hands were the same color as the skin of an eggplant, and their palms were the same color as the tanned core!

I would watch the girls' fingers as they chopped and minced *mulukhiah* greens until they became soupy. I would watch their fingers roll up the chicken in the bread and smother it with sumac for the *musakhan*. They were two dishes I never thought of cooking because they were linked to Hassan's death, and his *fedayeen* clothes stained with his blood, which his mother kept and would take out every so often to mourn him.

Before Hassan died, he rescued me from Dibo's gang when they attacked me the first time.

Dibo was an unusual boy, much like a dwarf. His legs were bowed, and his head was bigger than his torso.

A man's head on top of a boy's body. That alone was enough to instill fear in the hearts of children. He didn't just frighten us—his juniors—but people his own age, too. They chose to join his gang to avoid confrontation with him.

When they saw "Hassan the Palestinian" in a *fedayeen* uniform and the outline of a weapon on his shoulder, they scurried off like rats.

However, he didn't show up the next time. No one came to rescue me from that pack of "rotten" boys who used to chase little kids and rob them of whatever money, toys or even scraps they happened to have on them. It was all booty that they could brag about, and if they didn't find anything, then they would settle for beating the kid up or scaring him.

I was eleven years old, but that didn't stop them.

The first time, they wanted the "*ta'aysheh*" I had made from almond sap and an empty cartridge, and the second time, they wanted more: the "*ta'aysheh*" plus revenge for my having gotten away the first time.

There was a vendetta between us.

I ran quickly for home, reeking with the fragrance of bitter orange blossoms that fear had aroused in my sweaty pores. I heard one of them say to his buddy: "Go at her from the front." They were going to hop from one row to the next and reach the front door, which is why I decided to slip into the first place of refuge I could find.

They could have figured out where I was just by following the scent of orange blossoms, but they weren't so clever.

They didn't have that kind of sensitivity.

I only had five liras to my name—pay for helping my grandmother pick the bitter orange—or "*bousfeir*"—

blossoms for making *mazaher*. I would rather die than give them to Dibo and his gang and, because they were calling me "Sahbeh's son,"—not "Sahbeh's daughter," I ran like a boy, climbed up a tree, and jumped over a fence, finally reaching the roof of a room attached to our neighbor Bou Mahmoud's house. I reached to open the door, and when it opened easily, I remembered the neighborhood women's conversation about how Bou Mahmoud had fixed up the room for his son the *Hakim* so he could have a place to study and relax when he came home from his travels.

Through the opening in the ceiling, I jumped down only to be cradled by a sofa. My fall didn't only stir up the dust. It stirred up your smell, too, which you had left there.

I knew I was safe since no one would dare invade the garden of the neurotic Umm Mahmoud, that evil woman even Dibo and his gang feared.

While in that room, I wasn't just saved from the evil boys, but from the entire evil world. There, I stumbled upon myself, and I knew what I must do.

Then I heard the gang's footsteps receding into the distance. I looked all around to inspect the place. Daylight came in splinters through the window's opaque glass, but it was enough for me to discover the scary library.

I saw your desk—papers, notebooks, actual pens filled with ink and blank sheets of paper. There were folk stories, too—*A Thousand and One Nights*, *Kalila wa Dimna*, Naguib Mahfouz, Yahya Haqqi, Gibran, Naimy, and Maroun Abboud. Some were names I'd never heard of. Who were they, and why did they write all those books? And when? Was one lifetime long enough to write four or five books?

And what about you? Did you read all those books? A mind could not fathom that such a library existed in a broken-down neighborhood above a dried-up brook, perched on the edge of a cliff that the village nearly fell from.

The *Poems of Abu Nuwas*, the *Ghazals of the Arabs*, the *History of Arabic Literature*, *Platonic Love*. What are these books, and did you read them all? Who are you? If I read your books, will I know you? Will I understand you? Will I understand why you left my aunt? Why you left the country just a few days after getting engaged? And why you sent word to your family a couple of months later telling them to break the engagement and to tell my aunt and her mother those few meager words: "Wasn't meant to be."

Are you someone other than the person who caused my family so much suffering? Who caused the spilling of so many tears in my grandmother's house, and wounded the pride of the proudest among us? Are you someone other than the hateful, evil person who did not try to justify leaving my astonishingly beautiful aunt with any sort of excuse, which gave rise to gossip and rumors and left the malicious ones to multiply like mushrooms in the damp shade of our everyday lives?

You made us all miserable. Would I find in this room some compensation? Would you unintentionally try to reimburse me and open for me the doors to hidden worlds?

Who was this gloomy fellow? I get closer to read his name: "Dost…Dos..yov…sky…" I usually have difficulty sounding out words, and with a complicated name like this one, I would need a good fifteen minutes to take apart all the letters and tie them back together.

Dostoevsky and his masterpieces were what captivated me, followed by Gibran who had come at the appropriate time of adolescence, the blossoming of platonic love and the first love to enter my heart.

I concluded that Dostoevsky was your favorite writer because you placed lots of leaves and flowers in his books. Most were grapevine leaves and oleander flowers that dried between the pages of the books. I didn't know why you would do that. Why did you put flowers and leaves between the pages of books? To leave a mark? To express your love for the book and that particular page? Or to know how much time had passed?

Yes, you used to chronicle time with the leaves and flowers. That is what I concluded after a great deal of effort.

I started replacing your dried leaves with other leaves, not only so I could save the leaves you had touched with your own hands and placed yourself between the pages, but so you might find the leaves I picked and placed with my hands. That way, you might discover a trace of my being, which might lead you to me one day.

I brought many bitter orange leaves and blossoms, to the point that your library itself became very fragrant. It smelled like spring and *mazaher*.

If you were to come back one day, would you notice? And when you left, would you remember?

I took on quite a few of your habits, except for keeping a diary. My everyday experiences were too silly to write down. I never did anything important besides reading and cooking. My afternoon trips to the fields with my grandmother had become rare, and she no longer sent me to sell the things she had harvested or made.

What did all these books do to you? Are they the reason for your magical charm and obscurity, and your distinction from all the young men in the whole village—or at least the ones I know? Did you read about a different world and want to join it? Did you feel it was more deserving of you than the world of the "Hayy al-Hiffeh" neighborhood, and so you were driven to the ends of the earth searching for it? Will I have the same fate if I read all these books? Will a new beginning be written for me and a different life? It seems this was what concerned me most.

I hadn't yet caught sight of your diary or your photo album.

But when I did find those two things, I clung to them like a drowning man clutching at a straw.

I flipped through the photo album quickly: Tim being held by his sister, his older brother Mahmoud nearby.

Tim at age four.

Tim studying for his diploma. The Baccalaureate.

The pictures were black and white. You look handsome in all of them. Your sister Hind is holding you reluctantly as if she is afraid you might pee on her dress.

I stayed in the room for four hours, and when I realized someone might miss me and come looking for me, I slid your diary and photo album under my clothes and set off to leave through the opening in the ceiling. However, that plan didn't work.

I was already holding onto my bag of bitter oranges, so I was going to have to sacrifice one of them. I chose to hold onto the diary because I would need a lot of time to read it. The photo album, on the other hand, I could flip through whenever I came back to your room.

I snuck away in fear, as though I were carrying the biggest secret in the universe. I hid the diary between the sacks of flour, sugar and rice up in the storage space under the ceiling and went to help my grandmother distill the bitter orange blossoms that we had harvested.

After managing to sneak into your room, I would spend the longest amount of time possible before my grandmother and my aunt noticed my absence, and before your family noticed my presence. I would monitor the road, Tahani's balcony which overlooked your room, and the garden. Then I would wait for the opportunity to take off like a rocket, bringing something of yours with me.

I would return it after reading and take another. My greatest pleasure was when I would read in your room, knowing my grandmother was in the field and my aunt was at the pharmacy.

I read your diary over and over, looking carefully at your beautiful handwriting and some of the flowers you had drawn in the margins. I wished I could get hold of your diary in Russia. What did you write in it about the engagement? And why did you break it off? And what about that trip you took with my aunt to Sidon?

With difficulty, I swallow a huge thorn as I remember that fictitious and deceptive trip.

I am the only one who knows the two of you lied. You didn't go to Sidon. But, despite my strong childhood memory which is superior beyond measure to my recent memory, I didn't dare feel certain about what I remembered. It seemed better to just pretend the matter never happened, so the thorns of shock and jealousy would not ravish me.

It was a little after noon that day, and I was sleeping in the vacant area between the kitchen and the bedroom.

I was sad when I fell asleep because I had heard my grandmother say you took Fatima and your sister to Sidon. You went without me.

But in my dreams, I heard gentle whispers—something like music.

It was coming from that bedroom I have never known to be locked, but locked it was.

The place was filled with the smell of perfume mixed with nail polish.

My aunt's voice became audible. She was holding back a laugh which got away from her in the form of a gasp. Some strange sounds were mixed in with it, most likely from a man. Feeling I should leave, I didn't open the door. This was not out of fear, shyness or respect for whoever locked the door, but because I wanted to go.

I started collecting snail shells in the area around the house and eventually arrived at the brook. I raised my head towards the balcony and saw you two. You were holding her hand and looking out at the sea, while she was looking at you as if you were her sea, her unreachable sea.

Her hand was in your hands, and her gaze was upon you, with that dreamy stance. It became apparent to me later that you had frequently met each other and courted in secret. That day you were doing it without fear.

But I deliberately ignored what might have happened in that room where, when I entered it to hide the bag of snail shells between the blankets, I came across those female items—a make-up case, some bottles of nail polish and perfume, and a pair of white high-heeled sandals.

Later, when my uncertainty started tearing me apart, I was filled with regret for not having searched for evidence of what transpired in there between you two. When Fatima's flat refusal of all suitors who came asking for her hand kept my grandmother up at night, I was about to tell her that the reason was what had happened years ago in that very bedroom.

The day of Fatima's wedding I was distraught, as though I was sure she wasn't a virgin. But when the first week passed successfully, and some colorless weeks followed, I'd convinced myself the story of the locked bedroom was sheer wild imagination, or something out of a Latin-American fantasy novel I'd read.

Her wedding night was very difficult for me. I didn't miss her as my grandmother did but, with a strange and illogical force, I wanted for you to be with her at that moment. You and no one else. I wanted to lie in my bed and imagine she was holding back her laughter while you seduced her, with that beautiful music rising up along with the scents of fantasy novel heroines. Yes, in a strange way, I wanted you to have her. It was nothing new for jealousy to eat away at me. I had grown accustomed to it, and I could accept it.

If you were to come and discover the truth about me—that I had thwarted your meeting with Fatima before her fourth engagement, the one which eventually led to her marriage. If you were to learn I had something to do with beautiful Fatima's departure, that I had hidden her hair under a hijab and aided the collapse of her dreams of a knight who would carry her off to a better world. If you were to unearth any of this, would you be angry? Would it make you angry I hurt Fatima more than you did? Or that I loved you more than you loved yourself?

I will cancel the appointment or ask to reschedule it to keep the line of communication open.

I look over the text message and edit it:

Hello. I hope you are well.

My apologies, but due to an emergency, we will have to postpone our appointment scheduled for tomorrow.

Part Two

1

The sound of the rusty swing wakes me up as though it is my grandmother's hand waking me up to pray and prosper in the fields. And just as it used to happen on such mornings, I cover my ears under the blankets and go back to my warm dreams.

The sound of the swing is more stubborn than my grandmother's pestering.

I sit up in bed and look around. Now, while here, in Beirut, how can I be hearing Aziz's worn-out swing?

I don't remember when I heard it for the first time.

Aziz—the swing's owner—used to leave it out in the rain and the sun, from one *Eid* to the next, as though it wasn't appropriate for children to swing on it, except on some momentous occasion. He used to make them yearn for it, so they would spend all their *Eid* money on it. They would do so willingly, as though they—in their turn—also had their hearts set on yearning for it.

The swing was at the entrance to the neighborhood. However, despite its distance from me, and the impossibility of there being anyone swinging on it after midnight on this bitterly cold night, I felt as though the frightening sound waking me up from sleep was indeed the sound of the swing's rusty metal, but covered with a layer of ice!

I was a little girl, and the questions scared me. Who was swinging? Neighborhood kids or intruders? A crazy old woman or a *jinni* or a ghoul?

The sound would wake me up from one year to the next. I never connected the dates and their symbolic meanings, but they were always during nights of intense darkness and cold.

After Fatima got married, the sound stopped and moved to another house. It came back just one time, during the evening of your mother's death, when she had forced you to come to the neighborhood.

The sound was like the moaning of a clock hand stuck in place—like the movement of a child pushing a swing secretly after the adults who forbade him from swinging on it had gone to sleep.

Was it you?

Once, I decided to break off the shackles of fear and go outside.

I tucked my hands under my armpits, not expecting warmth because my heart itself was frozen.

It was a little girl with a short, disheveled haircut. The cold had left its red kisses on her cheeks and nose. Even her woolen dress knitted with fine needles seemed to be cold.

She looked at me and I understood what she wanted.

I went closer without fear. I pushed the swing, and she flew as if she were a feather!

She was light. Lighter than a soul!

When she moved, the scent of night-blooming jasmine emanated from her, so I continued pushing her with a joyful feeling that hadn't entered my heart for a long time.

Then she said, without looking at me, "He passed this way, but he didn't see me."

"Who are you?" I asked her.

"Who are you?" she replied.

"I'm asking you."

"I'm asking you."

She kept repeating whatever I said. Then her face and bare feet disappeared. But her woolen dress that had been made with love and affection kept on swinging gently.

The next morning the locals said that *jinns* had been in the neighborhood. They had been swinging. Verses from the Quran were recited for several nights, until the neighborhood folks felt assured that the *jinns* would not return.

I drowned in silence for days, speaking only to ask Majida to teach me the "wheat stalk" stitch, which had adorned the dress of the girl on the swing.

Majida was busy gathering up the laundry she liked to hang in front of our house, taking advantage of the noon sunshine. The knitting needles never left her side even during short visits. She didn't show any delight about my request, but when I described the dress to her in detail, she gave me a look of surprise and said that she had made that very dress for me when I was little. My grandmother had asked her to.

I felt my heart slow down before it stopped completely, and my soul departed from my body.

Majida showed concern for my condition and said, "Look here. This is how it's done. Watch me."

I inched closer and watched her work. She plunged the tip of the knitting needle into the strings of yarn, back and forth, looped the yarn over her index finger, taking her time, so I could follow what she was doing.

My turn. She handed me the knitting needles. It didn't go smoothly the first try or the second. In such situations, I would have deserved additional rounds, but Majida quickly lost interest. She got up to gather her laundry. I continued knitting; it seemed I'd totally ruined the wheat stalk.

She didn't get mad or yell at me. Actually, she laughed, and with an abrupt motion I will never forget, she yanked the knitting needles out of the yarn and started pulling on the long string, undoing the stitches

I had ruined. "That's not a wheat stalk!" she said. "It's ground wheat!!" Then she wound the yarn back into a ball, but the string was still crumpled.

Not only did she leave the smell of her laundry in my nose, in my eyes, she also left the scene of pulling my stitching apart.

If only I could yank apart the garment of my childhood and adolescence.

If only the stitches of the past years could be taken apart, so two new knitting needles could start weaving my life together with a different stitch.

If only I could be a little girl again swinging out in front of my house; and when the sun goes down, my mother could come and bring me home, give me a bath, dress me in a nightgown and feed me before tucking me into a soft bed.

If only I could be a pretty little girl with soft hair and two rosy cheeks. A young adolescent going to school having braided her hair into a ponytail. A young girl whose constant complaint was that every hair tie, no matter how strong, inevitably slid out of her hair because it was so soft, just like some schoolgirls who were oblivious to the blessings they were enjoying, and who so often made me want to pull the hair of every one of their heads, and pluck it all out so they would stop complaining.

Despite my wishes, just one thing happened: I got older. All that stored up fatigue made me feel I was twice as old.

As I knock on the door of my fourth decade of life, I worry a lot about old age.

It's not getting old and decrepit that scares me, but of turning into a copy of Aisha.

I have seen the way many women, when they get old, transform into carbon copies of their mothers and grandmothers. After fifty we start to resemble each other, the differences shrink away, and we find answers to most of the questions that confounded us since childhood.

That is why, at the moment of death, we become equal, and sometimes our stories become equal, despite differences in the details. Our histories resemble one another, too. They become mere consecutive copies made by an untalented writer who keeps rewriting the same thing in a dull style.

At the moment of death, we try to recall everything that has come to pass, and we end up with the following: We were born, we lived and endured suffering. We felt joy a little and felt sadness a lot, and our dreams were lost, then we grew tired, our waters ran dry, and we died. We have the same series of events and the same plot.

My aunt started looking like her paternal aunts when the first wrinkles appeared on her face. Despite numerous differences, I detected the genes of my great grandmother and her daughters in Fatima's face.

Aisha also started to resemble my grandmother.

One generation after another, we are here as nothing but successive copies, and with each copy, the original picture loses a bit of its purity and truth. We become more like an illusion.

When I saw my grandmother in the face of the dying Aisha, I was terrified. Will I turn into a replica of Aisha when I am old and decrepit?

My fears were confirmed when the doctor advised us—her daughters—to get tested early for cancer because it was hereditary!

She would leave us two huge inheritances despite her abject poverty: her cancer and her looks.

***

The sound of a distant *adhan* was trying to sneak in between the sounds of the air conditioners.

My unsettled sleep and my apprehension prevented me from knowing whether I had dreamed the "swing dream" or just remembered it.

That dream was more terrifying than the "balcony and bird" nightmare.

But how could it have been a cold night in the middle of this crazy heat wave that kept getting hotter? And how could that girl have been wearing a woolen dress knitted by two needles whose clinking sound I can hear right now?

"I am a soul, the soul of a bird," her final sentence reverberates.

Does it happen on this earth that we can see the soul of a bird?

My grandmother used to yell at me all the time if I complained too much. "Enough. Be quiet. My soul is the size of a bird's."

So, the soul had a size, but what my grandmother meant was not what I was searching for.

The soul is so small, it can sneak out of a tightly sealed grave, and so big, it cannot be contained by any place.

Why do we visit graveyards which have nothing in them but the bones of our dead ancestors, whereas their souls have been set free into a more welcoming place? Visiting graves is really a waste of time. It is only when we die that we truly visit our dead ancestors because we join them.

Sometimes I feel my death will be the easiest part of my life.

Despite the contradiction, it is a comforting truth. The dead will be there waiting for me, leading me step by step. Just like when we are born, there is always someone there to take care of us and teach us, regardless of the differences in opportunities afforded to each of us.

Was that why I stopped visiting my father's grave? Did I manage to forget the real reason?

One day, in the area around my father's grave, I came across a headstone with my first and last name engraved on it. I got scared and patted myself over my dress to make sure my body was still there, with me, and not under the tombstone.

That had been my paternal aunt after whom I was named, to honor her memory. Or maybe it was for some other reason having to do with Aisha's death wish for me? That she had seen a dead soul in my eyes when she refused to nurse me during my first hours of life?

After that incident, I stopped visiting my father's grave.

***

As it turned out, I only slept for an hour.

One hour was not enough to let my skin rest as the cosmetologist had advised, and not enough for me to discover any sign or guide about what I should do: Go say goodbye to the dying Aisha or stay here and meet you.

I take refuge in the sky as usual. I look up at it a long time and wait for a sign. It is meager and muffled as if choking as it slowly falls.

I say to myself, "If it rains now, I will cancel the banquet." But the sky hears me and doesn't rain. So, I revise my statement, "If it rains in the next half hour, I will cancel the banquet and send the text message."

I think of the raw meat we will devour together, and the nightmarish heat sends a sour taste into my mouth. What if the kibbeh goes bad? And the sourness overpowers the basil and marjoram!

I leap like a madwoman from one end of the kitchen to the other! Why on earth didn't I bring marjoram!!

What was I to do now? My feast was threatened with failure with a dish of raw kibbeh with no marjoram!

Do I have any option besides going back home to get it?

What if one of the neighborhood women sees me, when a week ago I spread the news I would be traveling to Syria with my girlfriends from the co-op? What if my aunt sees me? I reject that question because the chance of her coming to her mother's house is practically impossible.

What if her husband sees me with my plucked eyebrows and polished nails? Her husband who characterizes such women as having gone astray and neglected their prayers. When I replied to him once that many women who pray put on nail polish, since they don't pray all days! It was out of shame I didn't elaborate for him, not fear. But he did not have any shame. He called it "an excuse uglier than the offense itself!! Announcing to the whole world that she has her period!"

How could that man think that way? His words lashed me like a whip. "You're a girl with no upbringing whatsoever. No mother and no father!" Even my grandmother didn't defend me. She didn't say she raised me. She was trembling of him.

So, what about the marjoram then? My aunt's husband might beat me, defame me and forbid me to go back to Beirut! Where will I get some marjoram? Should I look around for a family garden in the vicinity? Do Beiruti people plant basil and marjoram like us? Or don't things requiring tender love and care figure into their everyday lives?

Shall I venture outside now for the sake of a sprig of marjoram? No wonder the first few letters spell "*mar*"—bitter—because when we eat it, we feel that initial bitterness. Then the bitterness turns into something which strikes the furthest reaches of the skull and opens the inner canals of the nose, finding its way deep inside the bronchial tubes!

My day and my banquet have turned bitter. What am I to do? Why on earth did I commit this crazy act of stupidity?? Why?

It's best to set the questions aside. I will get hold of some marjoram at any cost. For now, I will convince myself it is already in the refrigerator now and get on with my work.

***

With the appetite of a monster, I look for some chocolate I like to start my day with.

Due to my nervousness, I eat more than usual.

Dark chocolate, then a dark chocolate-filled cookie, and a cup of tea without sugar.

One hundred seeds from a cocoa pod were equal to one slave's freedom.

I mull over this fact whenever I eat chocolate. Then, when I swallow it, I remind myself what kind of luxury I am living in. People used to barter their freedom for the sake of these seeds which—without the slightest effort—melt in my mouth and flutter away from me for fleeting moments on the tips of my toes, like a ballerina.

I had hoped one day to mail you some dried roses, flowers and wild herbs: thyme, marjoram, sumac, linula viscosa, sage, and hyssop, and of course bitter orange blossoms, which I used to leave in your room and between the pages of your books along with the bitter orange leaves. But I couldn't see the benefit of sending you a package without knowing how you would react to it.

I forgot about the idea until a waking dream rekindled it in my mind. One night, during a thunderstorm, I was thinking about how, like a truffle, I had been born against nature and, during one of the strangest stages of growth, like a plant in the sand nothing senses except a bolt of lightning which most likely only found its way to it because it was lost. That was going through my mind as the lightning flashed before me, so I shut my eyes and felt my hand moving towards your mouth to feed you a square of chocolate.

It rained hard. When I opened my eyes, I looked for your mouth and the square of chocolate but didn't find either. I didn't feel sad at the time but happy because the lightning had inspired me to give you chocolate as a gift.

But sending a fancy box of chocolates was not a simple matter. In addition to the usual difficulty of making the right choice, along with my lack of knowledge about which flavors you liked, there was also my ignorance of the best and finest brands of chocolate. It was that same fear that prevented me from sending you my letters. I wished I could send a letter and get an immediate response. And now that I have gotten to know about the internet and email, my wish is possible.

Although I have only recently entered the world of the internet, I already have email, but nobody to send messages to. My list of contacts is empty. I wonder what your email address is?

I will ask for it tonight.

In creating my email address, I invented a name derived from yours: *Tayma*. The funny thing is that the entirety of my real name fits inside your name and always ends up as part of it, no matter the derivation. But the letter game tires me out. When I read that *thoum*—'garlic'—is a synonym for 'life—because the way it's spelled in colloquial Arabic—*toum*—spells the word for 'death'—*mout*—backwards, I tried the same game with your name. I turned it around and got 'Mit,' which means that your name is the opposite of the Arabic word *mit*—or 'dead', so then it could mean 'alive' or *hay*. I go back to finding a point of connection between us: each of our names ends up being composed of just two consonants.

***

The person who lived in this apartment before me did not leave any of his belongings behind except a small can of lunch meat.

Maybe he or she forgot it because it was crammed into a corner in the highest cabinet in the kitchen. Discovering it made my heart constrict. Having worked for years in a lunch meat factory in the Sidon area, I nearly vomit when I see those cans or hear any mention of their name.

The neighborhood women used to beg me to bring them cans of lunch meat. I would tell them the horrifying truth: "Lunch meat is made of gristle and skin and fat...animal scraps." But they didn't believe it. They went on eating lunch meat, unlike me.

My hourly pay doubled after a time but remained on the lowest rung of the pay scale. However, I had gotten fed up with my job and, when I got the chance to work at the co-op in Khalde for comparable pay, but without an annual bonus, I left the lunch meat factory.

For two years I worked against my will. So did Fatima.

No one believed she would work again after her first experience at the cookie factory, but when my grandmother fell and broke her hip one sweltering night, while picking some stubborn prickly pears, we were left with no income.

When one of my aunt's female relatives came to tell her the village pharmacy was looking for an employee, she liked the sound of the word "employee." But she didn't go to see the pharmacist right away even though the woman had urged her to. "Go on, hurry up! Before he hires some other girl." She explained to my aunt that the pharmacist had taken on some other work and, from time to time, needed to be able to leave the pharmacy for a few hours. That was why he wanted someone who could take over and sell medications in his absence. She explained it was an easy job—just read the customer's prescription and give him what he wants.

She went two days later to learn the pharmacist had made a spoken agreement with the daughter of a man by the name of "al-Samra". The daughter was to start work the following week, but when the pharmacist saw my aunt, he went back on his original promise, and my aunt became the pharmacy employee. And thus, the Prague-educated pharmacist became the prisoner of his own pharmacy, never leaving it. He even quit that second job and started coming early to arrive ahead of Fatima, so she wouldn't be alone with any of the customers. His jealousy began the moment he laid eyes on her. That was the cause of their connection, and the cause of their separation, too.

***

The smell of a grave.

Whenever I see a basil plant, the smell emanates from my heart, not from the basil itself.

My grandmother used to plant basil around the graves of her departed loved ones and, whenever one plant would wither, she would plant a new one in its place. She never stated the reason for this openly because I never asked her.

She believed the dead breathed and, since the smell of the corpses surrounding them was terrible, she wasn't content to just plant basil, thyme, and marjoram—she also planted a shrub of jasmine, the kind which releases its fragrance only at night.

As we were leaving one Friday, she said without turning to address me, "Tomorrow, when I die, keep watering them." I froze in place while she continued walking as though she were proceeding to the end of a black-and-white movie.

I felt a heavy marble slab over my chest like the gravestone under which I would be buried.

***

Her hand reaches into the darkness and gently shakes me a few times before I leave my reverie and accompany her on her daydreams.

"Hurry up. He's going to start the call to prayer," she says.

I get up half asleep, wishing I could finish my dream which most often features you as my knight. I perform ablutions like her, and with the *adhan* we pray the *Eid* prayers before picking up the bundle of myrtle, and we go on our way.

The cold lashes our backs, so we hunch over the myrtle from the pain. Our shoes click along, and the soles get worn away as they bang against the gravel of the alley. We don't utter a word, only breathe heavily, gasp for air or exhale moist breaths into our hands trying to warm ourselves.

It was the bereaved women, specifically, on a secret rendezvous the morning of *Eid*. They would creep out from their houses even in the harshest and most troubling circumstances. It was a ritual there was no escaping from—they must pay a visit to the dead on *Eid* at dawn before they could celebrate, or not celebrate—it was all the same—the important thing was that good faith and basic principles required visiting the dead first because the dead would be celebrating *Eid* in cold and desolate graves and, because they had died before getting their fill of *Eid* candy, cake and new clothes.

Each female visitor heads by instinct toward her destination. No need to open her eyes to see. The women could be blindfolded and still find their way for it would be their own final dwelling place and there was no avoiding memorizing the destination by heart. That is why there are no signs in the cemeteries despite the overcrowding.

We carry the bundle of myrtle, which the women call "*rihaan*"—sweet basil. After sprinkling water on the grave, we place the *rihaan* in plastic water bottles. Myrtle stays alive longer than other things, and the green remains shiny, but the strangest thing about its fruit is that it looks like small pearly beads which aren't edible. Nobody knows if it is poisonous, but it was saturated with the smells of the dead and the sweat of the bereaved women draped in black.

When I uncovered the secret of its fruit, I felt ashamed of those moments when I had tried my best and failed to weep over my father's death. I kept the secret to myself: its fruits are its tears for the dead.

Even the myrtle wept for my father while I couldn't.

My grandmother weeps over her infant son, and I shudder when I read the dates of his birth and death equalling a mere one month of life. The bones beneath this grave are very small, like the ragdolls that mothers make for their daughters.

We greet everyone we meet on the way back. *Eid* has started now, and I can put on what my grandmother's cousin—the family's "skilled failure of a seamstress"—sewed for me.

Her failure was barely noticeable because all the children were wearing what some other failing seamstress had sewn. They all resorted to them out of poverty, so we could not tell the difference between a good seamstress and a bad one.

I looked forward to the *Eid* money, the sweets and for Aziz to remove the chains from that swing of his which filled the children's hearts with joy. Despite its rustiness, it propelled them towards it, pushing and shoving, with their metal coins in hand. They wanted to swing and repeat the one song they memorized for the occasion:

"O sons of Abu Sharshouba! *Yobah*…Aisha the betrothed one! *Yobah*…And who will her husband be? Muhammad Amin…"

We had no idea who Abu Sharshouba, Aisha or her fiancé Muhammad Amin were. But the dream of getting engaged, for girls and boys alike, had been growing within us since childhood. It appeared the adults had been preparing us all along for a clear destiny: marriage.

Young boys and young girls—it was their duty to put their affairs in order so they could get married—the only journey available to them. As for going wherever they wished, on their own without a guardian, that would be a disgrace.

Like me, Salam used to dream of going far away, to Beirut or Jounieh, or an excursion to the Cedars or Al-Berdawni. She said she dreamed of getting engaged to a young man who owned a car and could take her to those places. On the topic of impossible dreams, in my spiteful manner, I told her, "Tomorrow the farthest excursion he will take you on will be to your parents' house…you'll end up just like all the rest of the married folks."

Salam's smile disappeared because she knew what I was saying was true. Aziz's swing disappeared too, without anyone knowing how or when. Some fancy and expensive amusement parks popped up in the cities, and the poor were left without swings or even Abu Sharshouba.

My grandmother didn't pour out her sorrows to anyone except the dead. And that didn't only apply to the mornings of *Eid al-Fitr* and *Eid al-Adha*, but every Friday before noon. She wept and poured out her heart, sometimes wailing in lament as she recalled her misfortunes. How could her husband's family have been so insolent towards her and waged war on her, even on her smile. How could her brother-in-law beat her after Fatima broke off her engagement to his son? She spoke of how that vicious woman attacked her in the olive press, and how the owner of the olive press insulted her and pushed her outside. She spoke of how tired she was and how she wished to be joined with them in their graves.

It pained me that she felt unremitting guilt and wore it like a shroud—that whoever she loved had died while she remained alive in spite of herself. She had suffered four miscarriages, all of them boys, eventually even losing her husband.

Forgetting I was there one time, she begged his forgiveness as she confessed to killing him with grief, for not giving him the son he had hoped for.

All this despite medicine not having been advanced enough to determine the cause of his death, and he most likely died of a brain aneurysm.

My grandmother had just given birth to her daughter Fatima two weeks earlier, and her mother was making *mughli* pudding and cinnamon and anise *einar* drink for her and her visitors.

He didn't wake up despite it being past the time when he usually left the house every day. They let him be because textile sellers like him worked during the summer and rested during the winter, spending what they earned from their travels and wanderings carrying bolts of cloth on their shoulders between Palestine and Iraq.

Before the noon call to prayer, his mother-in-law came in to wake him and spotted a stream of blood coming from his nose. Alarmed, she began pushing and poking him trying to wake him up, and when she turned him over, she discovered a stain of blood on his mattress, too, that had dripped from his ear.

***

My repugnance doubles when I remember that woman undressing. No doubt she was sleeping now after an oppressive night. Had she been undressing for someone in particular? Or for everyone? And had there been many binoculars aimed at her?

Mornings here have a different taste—of dust and car exhaust. I cover my mouth with my hand out of shock at the thought—will the taste of my cooking be different too? I dry myself off quickly so as not to forget myself as I usually do while conjuring up my fears under the water.

I tie on my scarf and open the refrigerator.

I go to the parlor and move the clock into the kitchen.

I turn the radio on. I wait for whatever song chance will send me.

"*Galbi habbak ya-l-asmar*…My heart fell in love with you, O dark and handsome one, ever since I was a little girl I've been in agony while my heart became bitter, went mad, and melted from jealousy…La la…."

It was a hit song here. Stupid apart from being good for dancing. A few days ago, one of my coworkers at the co-op said, "Diana Haddad has a new song that will make a dog dance!"

He was famous for his lovable personality and funny analogies. I didn't laugh that day because of something that was making me sad, but now—when I remember what he said—I smile as I imagine a group of people dancing at a wedding on some rooftop in the village. Then that song is played as a group of saluki dogs descends upon the square, start shaking their bodies and dancing with gusto.

A few years ago, the rooftop wedding trend came to an end. People started preferring wedding halls. That had been the sole occasion for entertainment for the people of the village before weddings came into competition with the more modest religious "*mawalid*" celebrations—for the birth of a new son, for surviving an accident or recovering from an illness. Families would put their nubile daughters—those of marrying age—on display, and the girls would show off their skills in dancing and coquettishness with feigned resistance at first and a pretense of shyness. The young men would show off their imagined handsomeness and virility, especially when they danced the *dabke*.

I know that girls' hearts would stop when the young men formed a *dabke* circle, not because I could check their pulses but because the *dabke* has always remained a man's game. Females who chose to watch, or at least those who were captivated by it from a distance, were not good at it.

I change the radio station hoping to find the horoscope readings, thirsting for a good word to boost my optimism. But all I find are stupid songs and news reports about catastrophes and disasters. They begin with the most horrific: hundreds of dead then dozens of dead then deaths of individuals.

Finally, something nice: "A decrease in temperatures is expected as the heatwave and spike in humidity begin to decline."

I play the cassette tape, feeling satisfied with this refreshing bit of news yet fearing it will be followed by some bad news.

It's the song "*Qalbi w miftaahu*—My Heart and its Key" which I like because Farid al-Atrash sings it in the film "Letter from an Unknown Woman." And I like it for the sake of the movie title, too, because undoubtedly when you see it, you will remember me, or you will remember the letter that you received from an unknown woman—if it actually arrived—and if you actually remember that letter.

My anonymous letter. What did you do with it? Did you tear it up or throw it in the trashcan or did you keep it? Where? Did you try to find out whose handwriting it was? Or did you never even receive it?

The difference is clear between the first letter I wrote, and the one I sent you. Even until now, I've kept every word I ever wrote—and unfortunately—every bit of pain I ever wanted you to cure, too.

Because I wanted you to read my letter, I worked hard at improving my writing. Dictation was my top weakness, followed by arithmetic. I got better at writing but not arithmetic.

At the co-op, I didn't need arithmetic. When I arranged the products on the shelves and put price labels on them, I would change the numbers using a machine I got from the supervisor. I wasn't required to write a single letter or word. I just let the price labeling machine go to work, and I would imagine you coming to the co-op. We would meet as if we were in a movie. You would run towards me in disbelief you had found me, and flowers and butterflies would be drawn all around us.

But the disgusting odors at the co-op slapped me in the face—whether they were the ones coming from the seafood store or exuding from the customers, I could not be sure. This was particularly true of the veiled women who, in recent years, had grown accustomed to wearing the "chador" as formal attire. I could imagine the thick layers of their clothing from beneath the chador, which itself was thick, based on the heaviness of their footsteps. At that time, I used to miss my grandmother's skirts and Umm Najib's embroidered lightweight ones, and their scarves that were as soft as the creamy top layer of *mahalabia* pudding, and their modest shirts which smelled of mother's milk and *mazaher*.

I kept their clothes in the closet which had belonged to Fatima before she got married. I didn't want to give them away as was the custom. They were the last of their kind in our neighborhood.

When I got better at writing, I decided to drop out of school.

I hated everything at school, and I was the oldest girl in my class. I had been late starting school plus I flunked more than once. This had caused me to be placed me in the last desk at the back of the class, where accusations against everyone but me were posted. This wasn't because I was truly innocent, but because I didn't have the strength to exert any effort, not even in the case of a brawl. I would be exhausted from the work I did in the afternoons with my grandmother—a job that never heard of a day off.

I would be exhausted and rather think about you. I submerged myself in my dreams. I would write your name and then cover it up with drawings so no one would see. I'd go on like that, writing your name and drawing over it, until all the pages were covered, and the desk, too.

When one of the teachers misspelled the word *ra's* (head) on the board, writing the hamza on the seat of the *yaa'* instead of *alif*, I wanted to correct her, but I was afraid she would reprimand and deride me, so I kept quiet.

When the bell rang at the end of the school day, the girls rushed to raise their skirts above their knees, dolled themselves up, and let their hair down. Meanwhile,

I rushed to your room to open the book that, along with its genie, was the first magic lantern to put a spell on me: the dictionary. It was intended for primary schoolers, so most of the words had pictures as definitions, which helped me a lot with learning to read and write.

I opened the page for the letter *raa'* and searched for the word *ra's* (head). There it was, written exactly as I had thought it should be. If only I'd had a tiny bit of self-confidence, I could have corrected that teacher and gone home, never to return. I could have taken a heroic stand in the horrible history of my schooldays, but I never possessed that confidence a single day. Even as I write to you, I remain hesitant and check the dictionary numerous times. I've never had full confidence except in the kitchen.

I dropped out of school and no one noticed my absence. My grandmother scolded me, but I didn't care.

Fatima's engagement to the pharmacist made my grandmother forget the matter altogether. My aunt didn't seem as happy as she had been for her first engagement, but nor did she seem as listless as she had been for her second engagement to her paternal cousin.

"The third time's a charm," Fattoume whispered to Tahani jokingly, and many other women repeated it menacingly. Would she leave the pharmacist as she had left her cousin? Had she decided ever since the

Hakim left her that she would get engaged and then break it off as a way of avenging herself—to be the one making the decision rather than the one sitting there sewing her trousseau while some visitor from her fiancé's family dropped by to tell her he didn't want her anymore?

Her suitors were numerous even though she was nearing her thirties. They dwindled to half as many after she left her cousin, since many of them figured the only reason she would accept a proposal was so she could break it off later. She ordered my grandmother to go to her uncle, return the engagement ring and gifts, and say to him, "Wasn't meant to be."

But my grandmother didn't dare enter her brother-in-law's house to tell him her daughter did not want his son.

She handed over all matters related to the fiancé to Umm Najib with full confidence she would do what was best.

Umm Najib was not surprised. Rather, it appeared she had been expecting this outcome. "I knew that meal was burnt" she said, as the darkness of the alley swallowed up my grandmother's slow footsteps.

The alley. Day after day it wrapped itself in layers to protect itself from the wind and the sun, just like a cabbage.

In her final days, Umm Najib didn't lash out against the long years of her life or old age or illness. Instead, she complained about the alley's decay.

When she felt her end was near, she deserted her house and her bed and made rounds visiting her relatives. She would stay with each one for a short period. She said to herself as she stood at the street corner not realizing I was behind her, "What's the point of wanting to die in my own bed? Why, did my sons die in their beds? Each one died somewhere else. What a joy to give birth to sons, they said. To hell with sons, and to hell with those that sire them!"

Her children died far away from their homes. The first died in prison and the second in some unknown place. His remains were never returned after he was kidnapped at a Syrian Army checkpoint. The third died when his brother sent for him to get medical treatment in Germany, and the brother who had sent for him died in turn in a horrible car accident. Is it so important where we die?? It seems that way. The old folks at Mary's nursing home were further proof, which Umm Najib didn't know about and didn't need to know about.

Once, I was making potato kibbeh for her. When I grabbed a bottle of olive oil to pour a dash of garnish on the dish, she yelled at me. "No!! Not oil from "*aamlawwal*"—last year. Use oil from this year. Who can guarantee we'll live long enough to enjoy it?"

At the time, she took a close look at a wart on my hand and said that she would reward me for the delicious kibbeh.

Perhaps it was her greatest talent: removing warts.

Getting rid of that disgusting mass required nothing more than a tomato and two long sticks of spaghetti.

She put the tomato on top of the wart and then started slowly plunging the spaghetti into the juicy fruit while chanting some short verses from the Quran for a certain number of times that only she knew.

When she was finished, the tomato had turned into a hard rock, and so Umm Najib said with astonishment at God's power that the Quranic recitations had caused the tomato to turn to stone, "Look…touch it…how powerful God is!!"

The person who had the wart must then bury the tomato and the spaghetti in the ground, and once they disintegrated, the wart would disappear.

This is what happened to everyone and to me as well.

In the end, Umm Najib died the death she had wanted.

She died on the road. They were taking her from the hospital to her daughter's house, but she never made it to the bed that was prepared for her.

I grieved over her death despite feeling relieved she died where she had wished. As they were burying her and everyone was begging for her forgiveness, I granted her my forgiveness, too, for everything—for having left me out of her visions and predictions and dream interpretations.

And I pardoned her for snitching on me. The truth was it had been my mistake.

I had underestimated how good her vision was. I thought if she saw me out on the balcony of your house, she wouldn't recognize me, but I discovered that she had been feigning poor eyesight to gain everyone's sympathy and get them to help her.

I calculated every step and every possibility except for Umm Najib snitching on me to my aunt.

I expected my aunt to strangle me for having defiled my feet by entering your family's house. I denied it vehemently and accused Umm Najib of being blind. It was the only thing that saved me from my aunt's anger and madness, she who forbade any mention of your name or the name of any of your family members, and not just in the house but in the entire neighborhood. Even when the neighborhood women would congregate in front of the house, and Fatima wasn't around, they wouldn't mention anyone from your family by name. If there was some anecdote pertaining to your family, they would indicate it only by nodding in the direction of your house.

After a period of neglect which lasted years, your father suddenly decided to trim the trees in the garden. He went overboard pruning and lopping off dead branches, as if he were taking revenge on them. The entrance to your room became exposed, but I had read through all your books and was thirsty for something else: your news, your clothes and your bedroom. That was why I saw being nice to your mother and helping her with housework as the best way to get to you, or to enjoy what was left of you at your parents' house.

I suffered a great deal from your mother's cruelty. She never liked our family and was the only one who openly showed her joy over your broken engagement. I suffered the same way everyone who got close to her suffered—from her crudeness, nervousness, biting sarcasm and her condescension.

I served her for nothing in return though she never asked herself why. Her arrogance blinded her to many things.

But I was much obliged to her for the compensation she had granted me without realizing just how valuable it was: tidying up your room and breathing in your scent, touching summer clothes you didn't take with you, your bath towels that had absorbed water from your body, your summer slippers, but the most valuable gift of all was an envelope I found with your address and phone number in Russia written on it.

I tucked it inside my clothes hastily while my heart danced inside my chest.

At home, I copied the address, and then I got rid of the envelope.

I wasn't planning to return to your family's house after making that most valuable catch, but my longing for your room took hold of me. Until Umm Najib snitched on me and all that stuff with my aunt took place.

I kept your address with me and examined every letter of it and every number. Was it really possible that, if I dialed those numbers on an international phone line, I would hear your voice?

I used to come home from the lunch meat factory utterly exhausted. I felt as though I was blaring like some overheated machine which had worked long hours and got turned off for fear it would explode.

I would arrive after suffering the difficult trip back home, which sucked the last drops of energy from my body, depriving me of the strength even to change my clothes. At that factory, I was a machine which arranged cans in cardboard boxes and tightly sealed them shut. The same job would be repeated for hours, interrupted by a half hour for lunch during which they served us the lunch meat, which I wouldn't eat.

Amid the melancholy of those days, along came my aunt's engagement to the pharmacist to lessen the reprimands of my guilty conscience, allowing me start thinking about something called "my own happiness." I asked myself: Why not be happy for once and send you a letter?

Without adding a name or a signature, I chose what I thought were the most beautiful expressions I had written over the past years and wrote them out in jumbled handwriting. It took hours because I was a slow writer and often flipped the letters of some words even though I was copying them. After much trouble, I finished writing the letter, put it in an envelope, wrote your address on it and, after my shift at the factory ended, I didn't go home. Instead, I went to Sidon, and with timid and hesitant steps, I dropped the letter in the mailbox.

I felt a strange sense of lightness and an obscure kind of happiness. Here I had finally dared to do what I had every right to do: reveal what was in my heart.

The next day, I woke up to a strong feeling of regret. What would you say when you received my letter? Would you mock it or think it's some sort of prank? Would you try to guess who sent it? And why she sent it? Would you make fun of the jumbled handwriting? And anyway, what did I stand to gain from your reading my words without knowing who I was? Would you think it was from some other woman, and then become involved with her? Had I managed to harm myself?

I regretted it a lot, and all I could do was convince myself you wouldn't get the letter, for one of two reasons: either you changed your address, or the mail lost its way. So many letters get lost, and so many others end up at the wrong destination! If my letter ends up getting sent to some other Russian citizen, then he won't be able to read it. He will throw it away and that will be the end of it.

How will I know tonight whether you ever received the letter, considering I don't intend to give you any direct indication of my identity?

I take out the chicken I boiled yesterday with some sticks of cinnamon, basil leaves, and nutmeg to start making the *moghrabieh*. I formed the tiny couscous balls myself, just as my grandmother had done the evening you left. I made them with chirping eyes and happy fingers. Didn't you say once that it's your favorite dish? I tried to fish it out from your mother when I offered to make couscous balls for her, but she didn't comment or mention you at all. But I imagine being away from home, as you are now, you miss this kind of a dish.

Did you search for its origins like I did in lands where you might come across Moroccans? I met a Moroccan woman at the co-op. I told her we love "*moghrabieh*," but she claimed she'd never heard of it. Instead, she pointed to a kind of dried pastry and said, "This is 'couscous' which resembles what you're talking about."

That must be what happened, then. We tried to imitate couscous, but we didn't succeed at twirling it into such tiny balls, so we created our own special dish close to the Moroccan one and we called it "*Moghrabieh*"— "The Moroccan dish."

It's deceptive for me to wear gloves while peeling onions and garlic. You might think someone else did the cooking and everything I'm building will be wrecked. And I don't even know how to work wearing these damned gloves!

I peel the round onions, which I spent a long time choosing, trying to find ones similar to each other because, after boiling them, I want them to float in the *moghrabieh* broth like a troupe of ballerinas— cinnamon, carraway, onions and chicken. What could be more wonderful than the smell of a pot filled with all these ingredients! The smell of goodbye, and of sad endings that came too soon.

When you sent one of your nephews to tell my aunt to come quickly, she was preparing the *moghra-*

bieh broth for you. When she came back, she was full of tears. She said you had gone to the airport and you hadn't paid attention to your flight time. That day, she refused to eat. I don't know if I remember that, or if I am retelling what my grandmother told me. In the middle of the story, my grandmother whispered to me, "Your aunt is like *'arousit al-zaraa'*—'bride of the harvest.' Have you ever seen it?" Then she fell silent as though she hadn't been expecting me to answer and would not have allowed me to do so anyway.

I had never seen it, but I asked her about it. *'Arousit al-zaraa'* is a beautiful wildflower, with a long stem, fuchsia in color, and the only flower that sprouts up between the wheat stalks out in the field. Its flaw was it didn't have a scent. My grandmother might have had that in mind, too, since in her opinion, and in the opinion of many others, my aunt was very beautiful, but her soul was as dry as a dead branch.

After that day, 'Bride of the Harvest' never again ate *moghrabieh* with the kind of appetite that dish deserves. In fact, she used to scold me whenever she saw the small round peeled onions boiling with the chickpeas in chicken broth and cinnamon and carraway. "I've told you a thousand times, I don't like *moghrabieh*."

I paid no heed to her complaints. I was too busy with a very important event I witnessed whenever what was in the pot came to a boil.

Something happens when the pot comes to the boil. It happens every time and once again during the day, every day, my whole life, and even after my life comes to an end.

After we die, our pots grieve for us. The cooking is not done by the deceased's family. Their relatives and friends cook for them instead because cooking is a joyful activity for celebrating life. It is not right for them to do it while grief-stricken. As for during our times of celebration, the pots rejoice with us and radiate with joy while everyone crowds around them. They spread the joy to the people offering their blessings and congratulations.

In the margin of one of your books I read: "Love happens every day but is always a new event." It wasn't your handwriting. I was fascinated by the enigma of the handwriting. Who, I wondered, had written that in the margin of your book? Or maybe it had been that person's book originally and you borrowed it from him but never returned it?

Love happens every day but is always a new event. Cooking and love are not two different things because their end result is the same, and their motive is the same. When you cook, you engage in an act of love. You make use of all your senses for the sake of winning your beloved.

When you love someone, you think about cooking for that person. In American movies and television series, the infatuated lover always invites his beloved to have dinner at his house. But he does this on the condition that he will make for her whatever dish he makes best, or the only thing he knows how to make. And the woman does the same. Characters in Arabic movies don't do that. Whether it's Anwar Wagdi all the way to Omar Sharif and ending with Mahmoud Yassin and Hussein Fahmy, the Arab lover most likely doesn't get hungry. Love makes him forget his stomach. He devises strategies to lure his beloved into some secluded place, not so he can cook for her, but to devour her. As for our women—we conservative ones—for the chance to sip up some of that blind desire for a man that is drenched in restrictions, we would amuse him with scrumptious dishes.

For years, I believed a woman got pregnant from a man kissing her neck. That's how it appeared to me in the Egyptian films which were our only window into stories of love and sex. The last thing we would see before an announcement of pregnancy was the man madly showering the woman's neck with kisses.

When rain kept people locked up inside their houses, whiffs of simmering food would signal to me that something happy was about to happen, something

I had so often calculated would never come; those whiffs foretold of love on its way.

I close my eyes to see your tall presence coming down the alley, to hear your shoes hitting the ground and the rustle of your blue clothes against your slender physique. You approach, closer and closer, but you don't knock at the door, perhaps held back by shame. I get up and stand at the door that has the small opaque windows. I don't open the door either because the color blue doesn't appear to me from outside, and there is no outline of you standing there behind the glass, nor any trace of your cologne.

I stand there drawing flowers on the steamed-up windows as I wait for you. I draw an entire marvelous field of flowers because you never come. The smell of the spices intermingles with the small amount of meat, the large amount of rice and the vegetables, the fat, the bones and the broth. My grandmother determines that lunch is ready, so she orders me to quit scribbling and go set the low table.

Because we are in the hot season, we can't watch over the pot or bear its heat, so we switch to making dishes that don't require a long time to cook, and if we do, we take the cooking out into the "lane" outside and take turns stirring. We have fun while passing the long wooden ladle from one hand to another. Dry hands with peeling skin around the fingernails. Standing over the pot with its heat and steam, all women contemplate themselves. It is a rare opportunity to delve into their own private darkness.

But that doesn't last long. They snap out of their lapse and withdraw from the darkness of contemplation. They alternate their gaze between the inside and outside of the pot, to find antonyms, synonyms and metaphors. One of them says, "Mmm...I made this amazing yogurt for you. You can cut it with a knife like a block of cheese..." Another would say, after getting some potatoes she was planning to peel, "Look at how magnificent these potatoes are! Like pillows!" And when my grandmother hands you her bread, it's "like putting baklava into your mouth."

When my grandmother taught me about bread's allure, she was handing me one of the keys of life with all its austerity and worldliness. For bread is wheat and water—two things with no flavor by themselves.

Water has no flavor while wheat tastes a bit like dirt. But with a dash of yeast, some water, and a moment of piety it swells up, becomes round, and touching it becomes like caressing cream. My grandmother divides it into balls and shapes it with her hands into something like a breast, which the nursing mothers of our village would, with total spontaneity, bring out into the open for their babies. They would bring out their breasts even in the presence of men, and the men didn't look or pay any attention, but then, all of a sudden, the nursing women started feeling ashamed! Until today, I have never understood how or why that practice perished.

My grandmother would press the top of the dough ball with all ten fingers and keep pressing until she reached halfway. Then she'd turn it around to do the same to the other end, halfway again, until the ball got spread out and was embellished with her fingerprints.

She repeated this until her fingers finished up the clever procedure, and then she turned to the rolling pin before performing the final trick: quickly raising the round loaf onto her arm and then "flipping it from one arm to the other," as she said. She continued the tossing process, each time widening and stretching the dough. Then she would set the special "*kaara*" cushion on her thighs. She'd place the stretched dough on it and pull the edges to make it fit onto it before, finally, sticking the *kaara* and the flat loaf onto the convex surface of the hot Saj. And then would come that intimate sound that I love when fire meets dough, and that tantalizing aroma is released, causing miracles to happen in the imagination, the intellect, the eyes and on the tongue.

She tosses the first loaf aside, hitting my hand reaching for it while imploring me to be patient and to wait for the second one because the first one is "the dog's share." The first loaf is always for the dog. She never gave me a reason but said her mother and all the women of the family would toss the first loaf aside and say it was for the dog.

Later I got an explanation from a woman passing through who said whoever eats the first loaf will lose her first-born son.

There is no doubt the first loaf is the most appetizing, and so many women would fight over it. For that reason, the woman baking the bread decided to throw it away and threatened them that, whoever ate it, would suffer the death of her first-born son—the worst calamity for any woman.

I understood a lot about life during my times sitting with the village women. They are not a clique, or friends, but sporadic women. They don't adhere to an organized or steady attendance system. One might be absent and could be replaced by her sister or her daughter, or some might turn against others and a new circle would be born of the original one, but soon enough they'd go back to the first bosom.

They used to think I didn't understand, but every time they talked about that unnamed thing, I knew they meant intimate relations. My grandmother didn't share her experiences on the basis that she had been a widow for a long time and had forgotten "such things," but one time she talked about her wedding night, during a women's gathering that was dominated by hysterical laughter.

They laughed for a long time over my grandmother's wedding night and the wedding night of every one of them. They laughed until they had tears in their eyes. As for me, I was very sad, and until today whenever a woman is married off to a man, I remember my grandmother's story and feel sad.

She was seventeen—skinny and bashful—and she knew her husband. Her marriage contract had been drawn up previously during the engagement period, and her fiancé had paved the way with a few kisses and stolen caresses. All of that didn't assuage her fears, though. Laughing, she told the women she would use the pretext of having to go to the bathroom and needing to pee whenever she was unable to bear the pain of the first penetration. The women nodded their heads in agreement and solidarity, and kept saying things like, "Yes, for sure, it's very difficult the first time…the flesh is stuck to itself…it's very tight…" I didn't understand completely because I was afraid to imagine it. But I could see my young, terrified grandmother running to the bathroom to protect herself from the pain that her husband, full of love and pride, was causing her, and which she had to accept with pride and shame as well.

Many people are overjoyed by the union of females and males. They delight and openly rejoice in their happiness while in the meantime there is someone paying the price of their joy with pain and blood and fear and excessive peeing and vomiting and indigestion sometimes. There is that woman whose flesh is torn and whose hymen is bloodied for the sake of the survival of the human race, and its victory over the arrogance of death and extinction.

I was a mute listener before deciding to enter into their world in my own special way. I was aware that soon, having reached the age of twelve, I would become a new woman, and I longed for that. I hadn't factored in the cost of the war, and I hadn't understood why people fought with each other.

The war was far away. Sometimes in the south, sometimes in Beirut. I was dangling in the middle, but I wasn't preoccupied with its stopping or coming to an end because I didn't expect there to be any difference between war and peace. Life was life. The days passed in spite of me without any hope for something better. Talk of the war that came from afar was like talk about the previous day's episode of "Abu Salim" and "Abu Melhem" and "The Amorous Adventures" of Hind Abi Lamaa and Abd el-Magid Majzoub.

Few were the villagers who continued to leave the village and bring back unimaginable news to us about the killing, torture, and kidnapping. The majority of folks stuck to the village and enjoyed the blessing of only having to hear the news. Majida's husband, who used to bring us fresh ground coffee from Beirut, stopped doing so.

The men of the village joined in on our gatherings. They were burdensome guests in the beginning, but I grew fond of them later, particularly when they made it clear to me that they could entertain the group either with the stories they told or the riddles they posed. They quarreled about everything, argued with loud voices, and disagreed about all but one thing: their love for Umm Kulthum.

Such different men—opposites sometimes—brought together by a woman. But she was "manly," and that was the great enigma of Umm Kulthum. Her homeliness, which was of no use except in one matter: putting a limit on how much they idolized her.

They invented a nice game I called "the second half game." They would bring cassette tapes of Umm Kulthum songs and put the cassette in the player on the B side without looking at the title. Out would come music from the second half of the song and they had to guess which song it was. It wasn't easy considering how lengthy her songs were.

That game taught me to exercise my memory, and it etched the songs of Umm Kulthum in my mind, verse by verse. The only awkward thing was the men's joining in on our gatherings happened to coincide with the development of my breasts. I tried to hide my secret under loose clothing or an apron or abaya, but it was a secret that could not be hidden.

I thought that everyone was looking at my chest. When I would go down the street, I felt arrows aimed at me from the sidewalks, balconies, and the windows overlooking the street, and from inside the shops and even the passing cars. The most unbearable part was passing by the coffee house. There sat the men I used to spy on. It was so bad that, even if I passed in front of their empty chairs, I would feel ashamed and couldn't breathe. I would wish for the ground to swallow me up, so no one would see me and tear off my sweater with his eyes to show everyone what I was hiding—I, the one who so often boasted to herself that no one knew her secrets.

When I saw that flow of dark blood, which had that strong odor as though it had been rotting and decaying for years, I was flustered even though I had been expecting it. This feeling I had become another person made me uneasy, especially as it came by means of this stain that was so insulting in color, smell, shape and feel. I had become like my sisters, the village women and my aunt Fatima.

In one of Aisha's crazy outbursts, she claimed that all the profits from the store wouldn't be enough to cover the cost of sanitary napkins for six girls. Those words stayed fresh in my mind, and I was scared if I told her that she would blow up in anger over "the expense." But I had to tell her because she was going to find out anyway. I chose—after a lot of thought—the right words for me and for our ever-stressful relationship.

"I had some blood," I said.

She looked at me and understood without further explanation or commentary. I stayed quiet a little while, tempted by a feeling of hope that our relationship would turn around, and we would forgive each other for the dark past—that she would sympathize with me like a mother for her daughter, but she ended the silence and my dream with a wrathful statement. "What do you want me to do? What are you telling me this for? Oh, I am so happy! Go home."

She didn't give me a box of Kotex from the ones she sold to the women of the village. She didn't ask me if I was bleeding heavily or having any pain. My entrance into the world of women didn't change the fact I was a cursed child. I was certain what happened to me was the exact opposite of what I had expected—a shameful and regretful action I must hide from everyone.

I didn't tell my sisters, either. I stole some cloth napkins from their closets and washed them in secret, since the disposable ones never entered our house except on one occasion. This was as a result of a suspicious incident when a young man was making a purchase at Aisha's store, and I was standing at the doorstep—hoping she would give me a piece of nougat candy or "*ras al-abed*" candy—but instead, she gave me a box of Kotex and said in a cold tone, "Take it home for your sister." I understood later what she meant, and why she intentionally did that in front of the young man, just as I understood why, with that frowning face and embroidered scarf she strangled herself with, she only smiled at eligible young men and the employed ones in particular.

It was awful not daring to show I was suffering from "period" pain, and for me to run out of schemes for stockpiling rags I could shred apart, to ensure Aisha wouldn't ask herself later how her youngest daughter was going to fend for herself. I learnt to deal with waking up to wet blood in the middle of the night and having to take my bedsheet to wash in the bathroom no matter how bitterly cold or suffocatingly hot it was. My grandmother wasn't aware of my situation. But one of her friends asked me about it when each of us was holding a huge pestle and pounding the bags filled with thyme leaves. "Well?! Have you peed on the thornbush, or not yet?" I lowered my face in shame.

My grandmother said to the woman, "I have no idea what you mean." But I saw it as a chance to disclose my secret and take the burden of it off my back. I nodded and said with some difficulty, "Yes...seven months ago." My grandmother was astonished and smiled awkwardly. I didn't understand the meaning of her smile, but her friend congratulated her. "*Mabrouk*...congratulations...Your little hen is open for egg-laying."

I complained to them about the sanitary napkins, and it seems that, in her naivete, that woman went and scolded Aisha, thus stirring up the embers between us and causing me to make my lifelong dream come true: I moved to my grandmother's house for good.

Aisha came looking for me, a rare occurrence. She came to my grandmother's house and yelled at me for telling on her. She accused me of not knowing "how to fend for myself," and expecting her to forfeit everything she'd managed to scrape together from working herself to the bone. "You want to clean me out from top to bottom? Why? For the sake of your beauty and good looks? Because I went through so much toil and trouble to bring you into this world?"

I didn't hold back. "Get out of here! What did you follow me here for?"

This time I hit her back as she had hit me, and when she got a feel of my strength, she left saying, "Go ahead and stay here, then! And don't you dare come back home. I wish I'd never given birth to you. You are not my daughter, and I don't know you!!"

I slapped myself on the cheek and ripped out tufts of my hair as I rued her ever having given birth to me. "I wish you'd never given birth to me!! I wish you weren't my mother!!"

I had been officially banished. Even though I had wanted that, hearing her issue the order infuriated me. None of my personal belongings were there at the house, and I had no feelings of nostalgia or fond memories, but I didn't want to obey her. I returned many times to the house on account of my sisters' engagement parties and wedding celebrations, but I stopped going altogether when Aisha fell ill.

I feared that if I came face to face with her on her sick bed, I would see her wishing for me to be her daughter again, so she could bestow her illness to me.

That watershed moment brought me closer to Fatima. It had taken years for me to come to understand her and forgive her for mistreating me.

Her transformation into a highly-strung and difficult to please person didn't happen suddenly. It was how she reacted to the loss which had thoroughly shaken her and continued to affect her even after her marriage and the birth of her two sons and daughter.

After calling off her engagement, my grandmother urged her to go back to school, but she couldn't. Not out to grief, but shame. She looked at herself in the mirror and discovered she had aged a great deal during the few months of the engagement. She wasn't fat, but she'd gotten bigger. She would look at her trousseau and hold up her wedding gown to her plump figure, feeling like she was already a married woman. Sometimes, she pretended to be pregnant and would strap a pillow onto her belly to see how she would look.

How was she going to contain her gigantic body beneath the blue school uniform? How could she shackle it behind a small school desk and expose it to the instructions of the teachers, their aides and their reprimands? How could she submit to the girls' questionings about her engagement, the break up and their malicious joy over her fractured pride?

Her pride hadn't been truly fractured until the day of her wedding to some non-descript nobody of a man. I don't know how to describe him since he doesn't have a steady job or even a steady name. At times he's Muhammad and other times "Haj Muhammad" and sometimes Abu Hamzeh. My aunt says he's a real estate agent, and his sister, who holds women's religious *mawalid* celebrations, says he's a "government transaction broker" in Baabda, while some of the neighbors say he's with "the Syrian mukhabarat!"

But I knew that he was none of these. He was simply a backward person who forced my aunt to wear a hijab without ever advising her how to pray. He hit me once because I wasn't wearing a belt with my jeans. He said pants without a belt implied they were easy to undo, and that the girl wearing them was asking a man to go after her.

My grandmother pleaded with him to calm down and leave me alone, saying I was just "stupid" and didn't mean anything by my actions. To defuse the situation, my aunt took off with her children, so he followed after them. I cried because a man like that had taken your place within our little family. A family that had lost a man who could protect them and have compassion upon them, and so fate sent them this savage of a man instead.

I had not noticed the likes of Muhammad before he raided our household. But I saw that such men had suddenly multiplied, like thistles which crop up in the summer and transformed into thorns that were difficult to root out. Whenever you did manage to pull one out. and stopped to catch your breath, it would reappear once again.

After that, my aunt no longer came back to her mother's house except by herself, and secretly. Her husband even forbade his children to come visit their grandmother. He said if my grandmother missed her grandchildren, then she could come to his house to see them.

His decision made me happy since his house was hell itself. My heart would start pounding whenever my aunt asked me to come help her with housecleaning or cooking, especially during Ramadan when he would serve banquets to his "brothers," as he called them. And I was prepared to help her on condition I didn't go near her bedroom. I had gone inside it once and didn't have the strength to do it again. It reeked of the smell of them together. The smell of their union—a mixture of his semen (as I imagined it), his sweat, and the scent of commercial 'oud incense he would bring back from Saudi Arabia. This along with the lingering scent of old rosewater that continued to emanate from my aunt's pores as she slept, most likely because of dreams in which she traded her sleeping partner for some other man. That man was you.

During my grandmother's final days, Fatima's husband sent two sheikhs to help her soul emerge in peace. They said they had learned of the old woman's decline a few days earlier, that she was struggling, and that God had not sent his mercy yet. I asked them if they had brought God's mercy with them, and which pocket was it in? They were taken aback, and their grimaces appeared simultaneously, as if they were an original and a photocopy. I drove them away with hysterical screaming and curses I'd never uttered before in my life.

***

It was eleven o'clock at night, and the April rain had stopped, allowing the silence of the cold night to prevail. Exhausted, I fell asleep near her bed without a blanket.

I don't recall if it was the cold that woke me up or her final cry for help.

I opened my eyes and found the clock hands before me, as if they were my *qiblah* for falling asleep. Ten past twelve.

My whole being was shaken up as though by electric shock.

I hovered over her chest and listened to her breathing, but all I could hear was the weeping of my lamenting heart.

I raised her hand, and the scent of orange blossoms emanated from her. The same ones that used to bombard us the moment we picked the flowers and threw them in with the other dead ones.

That is how the soul departs from the body. A candle is snuffed out, and the smell of goodbye follows. I saw nothing but darkness and memories of the light that was extinguished.

***

Today is Friday. At this time, I would be with my aunt on our way to the cemetery.

Ever since my grandmother died, visiting the cemetery had become my aunt's only breathing space, and the only outing her husband didn't object to. His involvement in organizing missions for Umrah and Hajj helped her. His trips to Saudi Arabia were the most beautiful event of their married life.

She might have gone by herself today. Maybe she was walking right now with her short, heavy steps as though shackled with hidden chains that only I could see. The distance I covered in one minute she would cover in three. I knew that marriage was the cause. It doesn't make a woman composed; it makes her heavy. Her soul is heavier than her body. I used to worry about her relationship with her husband, and how many times she had been dragged into performing her marital duties. The level of physical energy I saw in her could only mean hatred for her husband.

I never dared ask her about it, but I did ask another woman whom I knew had been forced into marriage.

"Tell me, Sanabel. How many times? I mean.... do you sleep with him? How many times a week?"

It wasn't difficult for me to ask her because she wasn't embarrassed to talk about such matters and usually didn't even need to be asked. She answered as if giving me a life lesson. "Look, men never get enough. They want it every day, and the woman has to comply...or else he'll say what the heck did he marry you for? Go back home to your father."

He'll threaten to kick her out if she refuses or maybe he won't give her spending money, or maybe he'll hit her. A disobedient wife can get whatever punishment her husband chooses.

I criticized her because even a hen would try to run away, even if she does end up yielding to the rooster in the end. She came at me with the following summary: "Pre- and post-nuptials, gold jewelry, a house and furniture and living expenses, and he feeds me, clothes me, and you want me to tell him no? That's his right. He paid for it out of his own pocket."

She uses her index finger and thumb to indicate money as she says, "That's his right." This confirms for me what I have long thought about my aunt's relationship with her husband: a matter of buying and selling.

But my aunt wasn't afraid of being thrown out or getting cut off from living expenses, or even being beaten up. Her tragedy was much deeper. She was afraid of making him angry and causing him to hit the children or mistreat them, terrifying them with his screaming and yelling. She would look at them and say how innocent they were, that they were victims. She had given birth to them, and it was not her business to burden them with punishment. I heard her say something like that at one of our relatives' weddings. She had been whispering to a friend of hers, and I was behind them, not intending to spy, but the bitter tone of her voice found its way into my ears. She pointed to the happy bride and said with a sigh, "She has no idea what she's in for."

As we water the basil, marjoram, and myrtle, I resolve to ask her about you—to spark up any conversation that has something to do with you. She won't scold or hit me as she is much weaker than any time in the past. In her misery, she might be longing to hear your name and recall memories of you. But I decide to respect her sincere sadness mixed with regret over her mother having died in her absence.

Despite all my curiosity, I never thought of asking her about what happened between you two when I encountered you in the alley that warm spring day. The dust from the road had made the air even hotter and heavier and the bitter orange trees were dripping, having been aroused by the insects' flirtations. Her cheeks had been hot from walking briskly and from the dust from the road itself and the buzzing of the bees that sounded like Fayrouz's hymns on Christmas Eve.

So many had wanted to catch her, and despite most families' appreciation for money, beauty was the primary motivating factor in choosing daughters-in-law. Many mediocre beauties and some ugly girls, too, got married by chance, or possibly by mistake, but they were not the rule. Families wanted to improve their futures and ensure beautiful generations to come, which would also ensure, in turn, that those generations could find a mate with ease.

Human beings are weak creatures that are terrified of being alone. They have always wanted to ensure finding a mate above all else. No sooner does life toss them out into its open nakedness than they start searching all around for a shepherd to look after them. Females believed that the function of the husband was to provide protection, and the males believed that the job of the woman was to provide care. Isolation, individuality, and independence were forbidden. And only now have I stopped being stubborn and admit how often I have been miserable because I was lonely. My attempts to make you my mate are nothing but a fantasy. One-sided love is a stroke of madness, a hallucination.

But I didn't have other choices. My life has been jampacked with other people's battles: my grandmother, Aisha, my aunt and her husband, my sisters and their husbands and their children—weighed down with misery that was much greater than my fragile body and my ugly face deserved. I wanted to turn it away from people and keep to myself, but that didn't save me from life's trickery and its evils. I was forced to go out into the world to ensure my sustenance, medical treatment and clothing. I never enjoyed the favor of a helping hand extended to me for free. Even what I took from my grandmother, I felt obliged to return.

I was grateful to my grandmother for never describing me as ugly. Most likely the reason she didn't say it to me openly was not out of consideration for my feelings but, because Fatima's beauty hadn't protected Fatima from misery, and did not turn out to be the blessing everyone had predicted for her.

Today, despite her lack of attention to her appearance, Fatima is still beautiful, but she failed to pass down that time-defying beauty of hers to her children. And with them, the genes for blue eyes and copper-colored hair will go into a period of dormancy. How long it will last, no one can guess.

The battle for my aunt had not been on account of a few dunums of land she inherited from her father, as she and my grandmother and even Aisha had believed.

It was her beauty and her youthfulness that were the root cause.

Her husband made her tear up all the pictures of herself from her youth—because she hadn't been wearing a hijab—and in so doing, if she were to die today, not a single piece of evidence of this treasure of hers would be left behind.

All her pictures got destroyed with the exception of one solitary picture I stole from the waste basket after her break-up with the pharmacist.

It was not easy for me to let it be thrown away. I got rid of the fiancé's head and kept the picture secretly.

During those times, when she would stand at her mother's grave with her mind wandering, I would be on the verge of telling her—when I saw how the grief was wearing her down—that I had kept a picture of her from when she was young. But I wasn't sure that would console her. The sorrow was too deep for anything to comfort it, and there was no response to its echo reverberating throughout the corners of the desolate cemetery, except silence.

It was good for her to cry, and for us to cry together. Each was for a different reason, but it was soothing—a spiritual cleansing exercise.

When I looked around last Friday, all I saw were women, and more women, weeping. That was our time to gather together to console ourselves before we died; it was the one safe haven that men had left for us where we could cry freely. At home inside our houses, we had to clean and look after the children, in the kitchens we had to cook, and in the beds, we had to do other things…where crying had no place and sleeping was not the top priority. I heard the women of the neighborhood hinting about how their husbands would wake them up from the middle of sleeping to do "that thing," which they never named in front of me or any other virgin. My aunt didn't talk. She had no need for that. I feel she suffered from something much worse than what the women brought up in jest that failed to hide some sort of fated grief.

I followed her and her husband one time as they were leaving my grandmother's house after a routine visit. He was moving along all puffed up like a peacock, and she was behind him moving slow-footed as if she didn't want to go, or rather to put enough distance between them to lose him and turn back.

I could feel her grief, and I made one of my malicious but just wishes: that her husband would die young.

When I thought about all the women around me who had lost their husbands, it seemed as if this had made their lives better. It gave them the chance to live as free women, and that was also one of the underlying reasons for marrying a man off to a younger woman. She could be a companion to him, a cook, a housekeeper, a child-rearer, and eventually a nurse and bedside companion. He had to die before her, clearing the way for her to live a few years without him.

When they get married, she dedicates her life to him and to his household. He, on the other hand, maintains a parallel life outside the home. He can continue to pursue some aspects of the same lifestyle he enjoyed as a bachelor, and he can travel, and he can even fall in love, get married, and have children outside his first marital home.

All the women I've ever known and ever heard of forgave their disloyal husbands, and everything went on happily ever after. But when the wife is the cheater and gets a pardon—in rare cases—no one accepts the matter easily. Cheating men actually garner improvements to their living conditions with their wives. It becomes mandatory for the wife to give him everything he asks of her, so as not to give him a reason to cheat on her again.

Majida, who swallowed the poison of her husband's betrayal, said that she overheard her father saying to his son-in-law, "All men cheat on their wives. You just happened to get caught. Too bad for you." Majida was shocked because implied in her father's words was an admission of his having cheated on her mother.

I wiped my hands clean of the matter in the faces of all the women present and said, "Let them go to hell! Why get married in the first place?"

Fighting ensued, voices were raised, and each woman put her two bits in. Then a voice arose with a different tone. "Tell me. Can any of you get by without a man? You'll go crazy. Try it for a few days and you'll ending up eating yourselves alive."

Umm Najib's words changed the rhythm of the conversation, and then Amal launched a bomb of her own. "All these women keep on pushing and pulling, but as the saying goes, 'No matter what he does to you during the day, when night comes around, you spread your legs for him.'"

I left them to go write that saying down, and I wrote Amal's name beside it and the date—as though she had coined it on the spot.

***

I was never convinced for a single moment my grandmother had truly forgotten the stories. Rather, it was the way she told them that changed as she advanced in years. Anything she didn't like, she just pushed aside, which made her stories happier.

I've done the same thing. Now, I tell stories differently than I told them to my pillow years ago. The difference between me and my grandmother is she didn't accuse me of losing my memory—as I had accused her—but of going insane!

"It seems you've turned into an imbecile!! Have you gone mad?? What are you talking about? That happened after…"

When she was at the peak of her mental acuity, I didn't push her to believe that ghouls were fictitious creatures which didn't really exist. How could I convince her of it now she was sure I had gone crazy and was the only one in the family to lose her senses at such a young age?

She would go on snapping at me and doubting my mental health. Then she would ask me to tell her another story.

I would wave my hand at her to show my irritation and boredom. I'd head to the kitchen to make her something more satisfying than stories. And there in the kitchen I would whisper to myself the story that I promised I would tell you one day.

"Once, there was a prince who fell in love with a young woman who came out from an orange and appeared to him. This stirred up the jealousy of his paternal cousin who had pinned her hopes on having him as her husband. The day of the wedding, the bride's lady's maid—in collusion with the cousin—stuck a pin in the bride's head, suddenly changing her into a dove, and she flew far off into the distance.

The prince grew ill over the disappearance of his bride, and he only got better when the dove came to nest on his windowsill. He left his sick bed and followed the dove from one place to another, and so his cousin ordered her to be killed in secret. The royal archer released his arrow, piercing the dove's white breast. She bled a single drop of blood and, on the spot where it had dripped onto the soil, up sprouted a marvelous palm tree.

The prince fell in love with the palm tree the moment he saw it and sat day and night gazing at and confiding in it. His cousin ordered the palm tree be chopped down and thrown into the river. There, the palm tree turned into a little loofah, and the river spewed it onto one of its banks. The prince didn't find the loofah, but an old woman did. She cleaned it off and used it to bathe herself. By accident, she pulled out the pin and the beautiful young woman suddenly sprang up before her. Then she swooned and fell to the ground. The old woman took her into her hut, and there the young woman lay breathing and pulsing with life as she slept.

Then one day the prince happened to pass by the hut and found his lost bride."

At this point in the story, I would get a smack on my head as my grandmother chimed in that she got pregnant from him! "She gave birth, and her infant suckled from her breast while she slept, and then, when the boy took his first steps, he failed to notice the presence of a raging bull. He cut off from his neck a magical necklace in which his mother's soul had been hiding, and so she came back to life."

I am the young woman whose life got suspended, and some of your flesh and blood will come to my rescue in the end. I am the one who was imprisoned inside an orange that might have been a bitter orange, and it is you who will set me free.

But I didn't know when that end would come. Year after year, it got further out of reach. And the worst part was that you were not aware of my existence or of the fact that there was a young woman pinning great hopes on you. You who dashed the hopes of family and friends and took off to the farthest reaches of God's earth, what we call "the end of that which God has built."

I knew Russia was far away, and even before the geography lessons in school, I tried to find it on a map, so I could know where it was located and just how far away it was.

I cannot describe the fluttering of my heart, and the way it chirped when I found that country called Russia on an old map in the principal's hallway. My hand could take it into its palm like a green leaf from a grape vine. My finger could touch the ground where you walked. My eyes could swim through the green areas surrounding Moscow.

I felt that I had accomplished a great feat by determining the location of the country in which you lived even if the rumors about your marrying a Russian woman were true, though I refused to believe it.

On sleepless nights I used to burn with a desire to tell you my secret but, because I knew what I was writing was trivial and not worthy of you, I had no desire for you to read my letters—even that lone letter I sent to you and regretted afterwards.

Did you receive it? Is that really your address I found while doing housework for your mother? The envelope had been left there carelessly on a table. It had the address of the sender on it and his name: Tim.

Tim. I don't know any other person named Tim. Lots of people wonder why your father named you that. Umm Najib told me the story.

Your father, like my grandfather, and like most of the men of our village, was a traveling textile merchant. In fact, your father and my grandfather were travel companions. They arrived in As-Salt and Jerusalem together. In Damascus, your father made the acquaintance of a kind man and they became friends. That man had a son named Tim. Your father liked the name very much and carefully stored it away in his memory.

That's how you ended up with this name, after someone named Tim from Damascus.

How I would love to visit Damascus and search it, inch by inch, for a man named Tim whose father had a Lebanese friend who used to go from one quarter to another selling fabric he carried on his shoulders. If only I could come with you to Damascus, so we could look for this "Tim the Damascene" and compare the two of you. We could go inside the Umayyad Mosque, feed the pigeons, and give prayers of gratitude to the Lord for bringing us all together. Then we could visit the shrine of Sayyida Zaynab and touch it, so she would bless our hearts and destine us to grow old together.

***

I soak the couscous in the chicken broth and wait for it to swell.

I quickly wash my hands and go into the bedroom to flip through the pages of your old diary. Shall I give it back to you tonight? Or have I become its rightful owner?

When you came for sporadic visits to the village, did you notice it was missing? Did you find traces of someone having played around with the books in your library, someone who had kissed your lingering scent between those pages you had once flipped through with your own fingers?

Between the pages of your diary, I found a wrinkled scrap of paper—one of those letters I wrote but never sent to you. It makes me laugh to see the handwriting—letters slipping and sliding across the page—which I was famous for in school. With a clear conscience, I would switch their positions within the word like a criminal who commits murder without feeling the slightest pang of guilt.

My darling Tim…

Do I know what love is? No one has ever loved me. At the girls' school, every girl had a sweetheart waiting for her, but not me. I have never loved anyone but you because I have never found anyone else like you. What is love? Yesterday, I was watering the snapdragons and carnations I had planted in your name. There happened to be a pile of salt, and that was when an idea popped into my mind: Love is when we see a cutting planted in some salt, and we tell ourselves it will bloom. That is how my love for you is.

What a disaster if you had received this error-ridden letter. Would you have been able to appreciate the love I have locked up inside myself for you? Would you write this quote in the margins of one of your medical books: Love is when we see a cutting planted in some salt, and we tell ourselves it will bloom?

It might make an appropriate quote for the margin of a scientific book—to decorate and freshen it up—just as the fresh coriander will freshen up the dish of green fava beans I will make tomorrow.

That dish doesn't come to mind without my thinking of Salam, the girl who tried so hard to be a good cook but didn't succeed.

Once, she brought me a plate of fava beans in olive oil she had made herself, so I could give her my opinion. It had a strange flavor, or rather, it was missing some flavor. What Salam understood from the name of the dish was that it was fava beans and oil, but she hadn't understood the secret to the dish, which was coriander and garlic. Coriander is a secret unto itself which is an essential ingredient in most of our recipes, the "stews" especially, but in moderation. Overdoing it would lead to the gravest of consequences. That scant measure of coriander was the key.

We've heard among our Druze neighbors it is forbidden to make *mulukhiah* stew, but the truth of the matter is *mulukhiah* itself is not the culprit, but rather the large quantity of coriander the recipe calls for. In every forbidden dish, I search for the coriander.

During the War of the Mountain, a Druze man used to pass by our village in a small truck to sell us vegetables. Our usual supply routes for vegetables had gotten cut off. We had no other choice except what was brought to us by the man whose name we didn't need to know. When the women asked him about *mulukhiah*, Umm Najib said disapprovingly, "Why are you asking? What does this man know of *mulukhiah*? Druze don't cook it." Then my grandmother added, before Umm Najib could beat her to the quotation, "Because the calf slipped on it." All the women laughed in surprise. I said to them in a calm voice that didn't pretend to be insightful, that *mulukhiah* didn't grow in the cold and mountainous Druze town of Baakleen. They all fell silent as if they didn't believe I was right.

I held back asking about it from one of the Druze women who worked at the co-op until I saw her buying some *mulukhiah* for her family. She corroborated my theory about the long-lost secret of the coriander. It's not completely correct that they don't cook *mulukhiah*, but many of them avoid it because it requires a large quantity of coriander. This was denounced for "arousing the appetite" or exciting desire (by which she meant lust), and for that reason their sheikhs warned it should be avoided.

A life without coriander? A life of chastity and mysticism for which I have absolutely no desire or inclination.

That colleague did not tell the whole truth though. She definitely did not know the secret of the even more dangerous garlic, and its having been prohibited in some societies because of the same bad reputation. She mocked us for believing the myth about the calf slipping on *mulukhiah*, and when I told Umm Najib about how she laughed at us, Umm Najib said, deriding me and my colleague, "The two of you are about as smart as my foot. The calf slipped means he fell by accident, he stumbled." Yes, she meant the forbidden fall. The calf ate the *mulukhiah* and thus committed a great sin.

Suddenly things appeared as plain as the sun. A cloud which had been created by our imaginations was cleared away.

I looked at Salam and asked her, "Where are the coriander and garlic?"

Her face turned red as she asked me, "Why? Was I supposed to add coriander and garlic?"

I laughed, having found an opportunity to show my superiority over her. "Well, aren't you a smart one! Are you kidding? Sauteed coriander is the most important ingredient."

Salam's failure in cooking was not the reason for her divorce. Most likely, she hadn't been given much of a chance to hone her skills because it wasn't long before she came back to her father's house crying and bruised, revealing the secret of her husband's impotence and that she was still a virgin. But the matter of the divorce soon transformed into a scandal when the family of the husband declared that he was the one who had kicked her out and divorced her because she was not a virgin!

Salam cried on my shoulder for a long time, swearing to God Almighty she had been slandered, and that she was pure. The situation grew more complicated when her parents took her to a midwife who discovered that in fact, she was not a virgin.

So, if her husband was impotent, then who tore her hymen? And if she had known she wasn't a virgin, then why hadn't she rectified the situation and gotten it fixed before the marriage?

That was a puzzle the whole village became preoccupied with, young and old alike. Was Salam a fallen woman, or was the husband who divorced her impotent?

I believed Salam without any proof. Even when she locked herself in her room and refused to see me, I kept on believing her.

Then her father threatened to kill her, and he would have physically attacked her had his wife not held him back. She begged him to give Salam a chance, and the chance was for her to see a gynecologist who could examine the hymen that was no longer there. The shocking LBC television programs about the rubbery or elastic type of hymen benefitted Salam's family, who were expecting the doctor to say that her hymen membrane was the rubbery type.

But it was not rubbery. The doctor determined that the hymen had been torn a short time before Salam reached puberty—roughly sometime around the age of eleven. And he thought it most likely it had been torn as the result of a severe blow. He asked her if she used to ride a bicycle as a child and perhaps had fallen off it. No, bicycles were not approved of for girls. The mother didn't remember, but Salam burst into tears. Her father ran to her with tears in his eyes and shook her by her shoulders as though he were shaking her memory to knock out whatever was stuck on the bottom of it. "Remember... Try hard to remember... Who hit you? Where did you fall?"

She said, with some difficulty and in a fit of tears, that there had been an incident one time when one of the boys tried to rob her of a Unica chocolate bar she happened to have. When she resisted, he kicked her in the stomach with his hard tennis shoe right at the base of her belly.

When she shed a few drops of blood afterwards her mother told her it must be the first signs of menstruation. But now she was finding out from the doctor that those drops of blood had been from the hymen membrane.

The question remained, even after the father believed his daughter's story, how would other people believe it, whose opinion it was—indisputably—that it was all mere fantasy.

Salam told me all of this and said, in between her sobs, that she now regretted all the chocolate she'd ever eaten in her whole life, especially the Unica bars.

I joked with her saying, "When he kicked you, didn't he swipe the Unica bar?" She wiped her nose, denying it. "No...I held onto it for dear life and finished eating it while I writhed in pain!" I tried to console her. "Good thing it was a Unica bar you were holding. If it had been one of those Galaxy bars that were so popular in those days, who knows what would have happened to you!!"

Our laughter mingled with our tears as we continued folding up the things from Salam's trousseau—which had come back from the marital home—and stored them away in some empty boxes.

I recalled the day when we opened all those trousseau packages, every dress and every piece of lingerie, a few days before the wedding. We never imagined we would be burying it all so soon with mothballs. Salam never hoped to open it up and put everything out on display a second time. She mocked the skimpy clothes as she folded them, her neck bent over her shoulder. As

I watched, I wondered what sort of inanity takes hold of girls when they buy these things?

The same question preoccupied my thoughts when my sister Manal was showing her "trousseau" to her "single" sister-in-law, whose mouth watered in astonishment at the skimpiness of those clothes, and in envy of Manal. Manal was envious of herself, too. She said that, because of her intense longing, she was scared she would die before ever having the chance to put on those dresses and wear that lingerie.

Most likely, Manal regretted it later though she never admitted it to anyone. She wrapped up some of her trousseau dresses as gifts and gave them to her friends for special occasions, assuring us that she never wore them once. Superficial passion melts faster than an ice cube in a hot oven.

But that was not the reason Manal's husband got himself entangled in a forbidden relationship with his brother's wife. In fact, the opposite might be true. After getting married, a man discovers this wife of his is a real predicament, a household duty, and that she isn't enough. The issue does not go unnoticed by the wife, and so she abstains from everything, including putting on her nice clothes.

Whenever Manal knew her husband was on the bottom floor of her in-laws' building, having intercourse with her sister-in-law, all she had the capacity to do was turn up the volume on the Future TV station so her children would not hear the racket. "You're my life, ask for anything and it's yours. What incredible eyes. I fell for you the moment I saw you. I'd do anything for those eyes of yours…anything for those eyes."

***

I write down the address of the hairdresser just as he dictated it to me over the phone because the address printed in the magazine is an abbreviated version, and I don't know the city well. I look out of the dining room window. I will stand here and wish you farewell with my eyes when you leave—in the event that you really do come—and I'll draw question marks on the windowpane.

I write your name and cover it with flowers as is my habit. And I draw question marks and exclamation points in the remaining white space on the paper.

I have three big questions.

The number three is legendary. In all the stories, there are always three poor girls, and the third one is the heroine. And there are three cryptic riddles the hero must solve, and three tests for him to pass. My grandmother didn't know the story of Cinderella or Snow White, but I knew Cinderella was the third girl in the household and that she goes to the Prince's ball three times, and on the third time she leaves her shoe behind. I also knew Snow White is subjected to three murder attempts by the witch. Al-Shater Hassan was the son of the third young woman, and he goes on three journeys to the land of the ghouls.

The ghoul's daughter is his third daughter, and the ghoul places three unbearable conditions on the prince who comes to ask for her hand in marriage. Likewise, there's the young woman whose two sisters feed her pregnancy-inducing eggs, causing her to become pregnant and having to run away for fear of her father's anger and her mortal shame. What a horrible fate! A young virgin eats an egg with a spell on it and gets pregnant, and she flees before her father discovers her swelling belly. She flees barefooted and the thorns cause her feet to bleed! She flees into the desolate wild world, and the jackals chase after her. Stumbling is simply not an option.

This story takes a detour at the part with the "three riddles" and intersects with my story, which ends with three questions: Why did you break off your engagement? Why does Aisha hate me? And why didn't I die when I fell from the balcony?

You hold one of the answers, Aisha holds another, and God holds the third.

This is why I will never find peace of mind before I die. Aisha will never answer, and no matter how hard I look for excuses for what she destroyed in my life, I won't find any. And you most likely will not remember, but if you do, you will evade the question. And if you don't evade the question and do tell the truth, it won't do me any good. As for God, years have passed since our estrangement began. He left me on my own, threatening we would meet in another life I know nothing about except that it has the same scent as Friday mornings.

The scent of watered basil and marjoram…

Yes, that's right! The marjoram that I planted around my grandmother's grave. I will sneak over there and pick some, assuming my aunt has been watering it during this heat wave.

That would be another disaster! After taking the risk of going there, I might not find the marjoram plant alive.

2

I dreamed of one day becoming a doctor like you, but I got so frustrated I ended up forgetting all about it.

I would repeat the phrase in my heart, "Doctor Bint Sahbeh," and the echo would come back, reverberating like the howling of jackals lost in the night of "the brook," choking and gagging with mockery. And then, how was I to study medicine knowing full well my tragic experience with arithmetic and mathematics?

That is why I concentrated on dreaming of traveling to you. I wanted to work day and night to make enough money to travel to Moscow and find my way to the address written on that old envelope, which I know by heart and repeat every night to remind myself to never forget the dream: a trip to Moscow.

That dream enticed me, along with other crazy dreams, from the moment I found your diary. But over the years, that dream became the strongest and greatest of all.

I swept aside all obstacles in front of it and pushed away all other dreams that might lessen its splendor. It topped all my priorities. And whenever I would count up my savings, I would tell the money, as I kissed it, that it was going to take me to Moscow. Then I'd hide it up in the ceiling storage area inside the barrel of flour that no one dipped into but me.

Now, all that money, along with the gold pound, is going towards banquet expenses—rent for the apartment, and the cost of furnishing it, groceries for the dinner, the clothes, the coiffeur, the cosmetologist, transportation, and the white sandals, too. Now, I don't have to travel or go through the trouble of getting a visa. As soon as I heard about your scheduled trip here to Lebanon, I embarked upon this plan of mine and mustered enough courage to call you on the phone and ask you when you planned to be in Beirut. I did all this so you could participate in a statistical study being conducted by a research company on "The Generation of Students in Russia during the Lebanese War Period." I planned it out well and chose my words carefully, writing them down on a piece of paper. I started reading from it as I made the call to you with my heart and stomach exploding in terror and adoration. Sweat poured from me, and fire emerged from my cheeks.

Fortunately, I also wrote down the time you specified on the phone because I wouldn't have remembered the number: the day and the month. Rather than giving me the name of the month, you gave me numbers: 3—4.

The third of April. That was the date you would arrive, and the seventh was the date when we would meet.

At last, Friday's luck was going to change, after having been stuck on the cemetery what with the wailing, and the sight of women all wrapped in black, carrying aromatic plants and pails of water to pour on the graves of their sons, husbands and fathers. The son first because he was younger, then the husband, then the father. Men die in droves, and in a hurry. I noticed that about our family's deceased before checking the names on the headstones—my grandfather, my father, my uncle Shibl and three male fetuses before him. They were quick to go downhill. Quick to surrender to death.

***

I never lived with a man. During the short period of my life when my father was in it, he was practically never there. He spent all his time between hunting and the coffee house. Around midnight, I would hear the sound of his key and the creaking of the door as he opened it. At the crack of dawn, he would be up again, headed for another day of hunting, hopefully with better luck this time. He would make up for lost sleep in the afternoon, before leaving again for the coffee house to sell the fruits of his hunting expedition, and to play cards.

My maternal grandfather died no more than two weeks after the birth of my aunt Fatima, and my paternal grandfather died one year before I was born. When I thought about males dying quickly, I would worry about you. Even your father died before your mother.

As for me, I hadn't prevailed over death because I was strong and resilient, but because Mary had taken pity on my grandmother and gave her some money to buy baby formula. Years later, Mary gave me one other sweet thing.

I had gone with my grandmother to the nursing home because, at the end of her shift, she was going to take me to the doctor to have my eyes examined. The teachers had been complaining I wasn't copying things correctly from the board, and I didn't read well.

Mary was kind and beautiful and more…She gave me a piece of Ooh La La nougat candy I used to see advertised on Télé Liban; I knew the jingle by heart: "*Ooh La La*…The yummiest nougat with *chocolaaah*."

Mary disappeared after the Mountain War. A whole year went by while my grandmother asked about her until we finally found out she had settled in Jounieh with her brother. Years later, we heard she followed her nephews to Australia.

A dream she was, that Mary—a giant who burst forth, gave me chocolate nougat candy, and then vanished.

I imagine her in that shirt of hers with the short sleeves cut off at the armpits, running and crying as she gets into a car. And I say it's okay if she's forgotten the nougat candy in her office since the old folks will certainly enjoy it.

We never found out where the old folks ended up. What had the combatants done with them?

My grandmother wasn't concerned about the patients so much as the severance of her meager income. The main source of our daily sustenance got cut off, but the taste of nougat and chocolate remained forever in my mouth. As for the eye doctor's examination, he determined my vision was excellent; and he couldn't say exactly, but if my problem at school didn't stem from my vision, then it must stem from some other place, the depths of which no one had fathomed, yet.

The only happy one was Fatima. The war had forced her mother to quit her lowly laundry washing job, but what had made Fatima happy, made me and my grandmother miserable. It forced us to double our efforts in the fields, particularly the production of olive oil soap and orange blossom water. Both of these had become the family trade and had earned us a reputation in the surrounding villages, all of which led my grandmother to hire her niece.

She abandoned the notion of begging me for help once and for all when she realized I had a lot of Fatima's defiance and a half-blackened heart. This hadn't occurred to her before.

Instead of working with her, burning my skin on the tar and watching the drops of orange blossom water as they dripped, I would sit for hours reading, writing, tearing my writing to shreds and dreaming of you. I imagined myself as a doctor in the hospital where you work—us assisting each other in the operating room, having coffee together in the cafeteria, just as I had seen the doctors do at the hospital when my oldest sister gave birth to her first child. I never imagined a person that size could exist. I could cover him up completely with the palm of my hand.

His father named him Walid after the Druze leader, Walid Jumblatt. Before Walid was one week old, his mother fled with him, Aisha and my sisters to the South to escape the Mountain War. "The youngest exiled political leader," I muttered to myself.

I stayed because I was afraid. What I told them: "I'll stay for grandmother's sake," wasn't true.

My grandmother was being genuine when she asked, "Who is going to look after the olives? Who is going to feed the chickens? And what if the house gets set on fire?"

But I was lying. I didn't stay with her out of love for her, but because I was afraid to get into a car and travel on the roads. What if they attacked us on the road? What if they slaughtered us, like in the stories I'd heard about others who got slaughtered like sheep?

I looked around for my aunt, but she had caught up with Aisha and crammed herself into the car.

The neighborhood became completely desolate. The only people left were old folks like my grandmother who would come up with any excuse they could find as a reason to stay.

I regretted it, though, and blamed my grandmother. I even cursed her under my breath. The sounds of bombs grew stronger and closer, and the time between one and the next got shorter.

"I'm going to die," I kept repeating to myself. I found the kitchen to be safer than any other place. I crouched in the innermost corner and covered my ears with the palms of my hands. That day, some shrapnel fell into the brook. No one got hurt except for my grandmother's conscience as she wished she had shoved me into the car with Fatima, whether I liked it or not.

To this day, I have no idea how word got around that I was hiding in the kitchen! But that cursed night, everyone who had stayed behind in the neighborhood headed for the kitchen when the bombs and cannons went berserk. The kitchen turned into a refuge for people I knew and for people I'd never seen in my life!

That night filled me with terror for many long years, not because of the bombs and all the frightened bodies packed into close quarters stinking dreadfully of the sweat pouring from them. It was because of a young woman neither I nor anyone else from the neighborhood knew.

She didn't say a word. She was around ten years old, so I was about five years older than her. Despite her childlike face, her body was womanly. She sat with her knees hugged to her chest beneath her thick cotton dress. The women asked her about her parents. "Whose daughter are you?" She didn't answer. They showered her with questions, but still she didn't answer. One of them said that maybe she was mute, and another woman's husband said maybe she'd lost her ability to speak and hear that night, due to the terrifying events taking place.

She didn't budge or look up at whoever was questioning her, until everyone became convinced that she was deaf and dumb.

After an hour passed, she spoke. She asked for the bathroom. My grandmother showed her. She went into the bathroom and lots of whispering about her ensued. Who was she? Whose daughter? How did she get here? Who has seen her before?

But her scream from inside the bathroom silenced everyone. My grandmother got up to check on her.

My grandmother opened the bathroom door, and I felt a dagger cleave my forehead in two. A jolt of electricity zapped my brain.

The girl was standing with her dress raised, pulled away from her legs. Her underwear, which was dangling around her knees, was stained with blood. She let out another blood curdling scream, prompting the men—even before the women—to go see what was happening. And they saw. All of them, without exception.

She had screamed thinking she had been hit by a bomb, but my grandmother checked her body carefully and reassured her.

My grandmother set the kitchen refugees at ease with some obscure words only grown-ups would understand. She locked the bathroom door to be alone with the girl whose childlike facial features had been transformed by fear into the wrinkled-up face of someone who had looked directly into the sun.

My grandmother came out of the bathroom holding onto the girl. She sat her down, consoled her with kind words, and gave her to drink from the "chalice of fear" engraved with Quranic verses, saying, "There's nothing to worry about, dear…It's nothing…nothing…all girls have this…it was bound to happen."

I felt sorry for the girl's predicament, to be scandalized that way in the middle of that crowd, but I couldn't handle sitting with her. And I couldn't bear the smell of her first menstrual blood. So, I went outside to get some new air even if it was thick with the smell of gunpowder.

She was one of the girls I considered worse off than me. So many strangers, women and men alike, had witnessed the onset of that girl's sexual maturity, which was supposed to be the most sacred of women's secrets. And now she had entered the world of women, and her mother would forbid her from playing with her girlfriends and from passing in front of boys. Terror had hijacked her childhood. The bombs which had been raining down on our heads caused her to bleed without being struck by a single bullet.

I tried hard to forget her, wishing she would disappear the same way she had appeared. And then, she did—for two whole years.

When the warring fronts quietened down, and it was rumoured the Mountain War was over, we all went back to our work and our lives—only then did she reappear. She became, on the contrary, the girl I came across most often whenever I went outside the neighborhood.

I would run into her at least once a day—on the street, on busses, or in taxis though we never spoke, and I never asked anyone about her or even what her name was. She never looked at me, either. She had a good talent for disregarding others. Her eyes never once made contact with mine, and I, in turn, tried to ignore her presence as well, assuring myself she hadn't seen me.

One time, we ended up in a taxi together. She had taken the front seat as usual, paying the price of two passengers on account of her weight and shyness about having anyone crammed up against the heavy rolls of fat that dangled from her body. When she got out, the woman sitting beside me whispered a comment to her daughter while holding back a laugh, "*Ghazaala*"!

She was mocking her, using that description—an elegant gazelle—the exact opposite of what she really was, to make her daughter laugh.

I felt sorry for her, and then for myself. Me too. For sure, when I get out of the taxi, the passengers and the driver will make fun of me. Of my eyebrows? Of my ugliness? Of my embarrassment inside these cheap clothes I wear? They had a lot of choices.

Then the fat young woman disappeared completely.

I was happy to fold up my memories of her. I forgot about her for an entire decade.

That was until one Friday when I walked past a new gravestone at the cemetery and read the name of the deceased: Ghazaala Muhammad Badeea, b. 1975. I felt certain it was her. She must have been pretending to be deaf out of shame about her name. Perhaps that night in the kitchen, she had run away from home after fighting with her parents about her name and her weight. Now, here she was, lying beneath that gravestone and crying in terror all alone, not finding anyone who would offer her the "chalice of fear" and a drop of water to drink.

I used to water her grave from time to time, until one time when I ran into a woman who was lamenting over the grave, and so I asked her about the deceased.

She told me her story.

I was shocked. That woman in the taxi had not been calling her a name to make her daughter laugh. She had been calling her by her real name.

Ghazaala.

The 'gazelle' whose first drops of blood I had witnessed kept getting fatter and fatter until diabetes shed all her blood.

Her own name had killed her. Despair had gotten to her. The more the people called her 'Gazelle', the fatter and fatter she got.

She disappeared from the streets and public transportation to go live on the road to my grandfather and uncle's grave before my grandmother joined them.—that same road I will traverse every *Eid* and every Friday until my life melts away, drop by drop, and I am extinguished when it reaches the end.

***

I get nervous when I count how many hours are left. Five hours. How can I hold myself together through them? How can I make them be happy hours, calm hours?

I look at my notebook to double-check the time of my appointment with the coiffeur. My relationship with clocks and clock hands has been bad for such a long time. It's the same with numbers which I cannot decipher without exerting effort.

Four o'clock. Yes, that was the time I requested. I could get back home by five to put the finishing touches on the banquet and to get into my dress and high heels. Before four, I have a lot to do, but I feel as though I've forgotten how to cook! I'm like a schoolgirl again—waiting for the exam questions.

Will everything go according to plan? According to what I wrote in my notebook? So that I wouldn't make any mistakes in the procedures, forget any of the steps, or have the time get away from me? I wrote the time on one side of the paper and wrote beside it what I was supposed to do. Forty-eight hours, two days. Three-quarters of them had already gone by. The last number was seven o'clock this evening. I didn't write any other numbers after that. What will I do at eight, nine, and ten—after you leave—if it turns out you come? The dinner won't last more than two hours. And after the two hours, will I be washing dishes and thinking about tomorrow? Deciding between going back to the village, staying here, or possibly going to the beach like the thousands of people around me, that skinny woman being one of them.

How can I guarantee this time I will do a good job cooking and there won't be any mistakes? How can I guarantee all the ingredients will be in just the right amounts as usual? When I am the one who never uses measuring tools or weighing scales, feeling it with my fingers when adding a dash here and a dash there. I don't measure things with numbers. I let my fingers, hands and eyes do their thing and estimate intuitively—the salt, the spices, and I even measure the water and other liquids by lifting them to gauge their weight.

I have never been able to give the recipes for dishes I'm good at making. The other women thought I was being mean and holding back secrets from them. I would try to explain it was based on how I felt it, not how I had learned it—a little dash here, or a big dash there—a handful of flour, two handfuls of coriander. Would it have worked if their hands were like my hands and their fingers, particularly the index finger, thumb, and pinky, were like my fingers? I was not being mean at all—just oblivious to measurements and numbers.

At my father's house, Aisha didn't cook. She spent all her time at the store. My grandmother on my father's side was in charge of the cooking. She would send up food from her house on the first floor to our house on the second floor. While this was going on, Aisha stayed in the store on the bottom floor of the building, smelling all the aromas emanating from her mother-in-law's kitchen, and guessing what she was cooking. This was all because communication between the two women was virtually nonexistent.

During my first years of life, Aisha kept me with her at the store. It was damp and musty because the only source of light or air was the doorway. She wouldn't close the door in the cold of winter to avoid the darkness, which is why I got sick a lot. She didn't make any effort to treat my illness because, as she boasted in front of the women, she refused to allow one pill of Panadol to enter her house. She let her children recover on their own to build up immunity.

Aisha's store was below street level. You had to duck down and ponder every step as you made your way down two crumbling stairs and through the low doorway. That gloomy room was never spared from floods except by a miracle. I could feel how low the ceiling was and feared it would collapse right on top of my heart by means of some plot Aisha herself had cooked up. Everything about that woman, even the walls between which she lived out most of her life, wanted to get rid of me.

Aisha had gotten pregnant with me by mistake, but she didn't do anything to improve the matter.

She didn't go to some sheikh as she had done when she got pregnant with Zalfa. And she didn't try to induce a miscarriage as had happened with that unidentified fetus she'd lost.

Likewise, she abandoned the old beliefs about certain vegetables which hadn't been successful for her with the previous five births, like eating cabbage but refraining from lettuce and favoring salty foods over sweets.

One woman tried to take her to a sheikh *"waasel"*— who has supernatural connections for helping in such matters, but her experience with a previous woman sheikha convinced her of the benefits of staying put at the store.

When she got pregnant with Zalfa, she went to the Beqaa with her barren sister-in-law, Nabiha. Each of them paid a lot of money in return for two little amulets.

That sheikha's formula was very strange. She gave them the two amulets and told Aisha to pee on her amulet and told Nabiha to have her husband pee on her amulet so she would get pregnant. Flustered, Nabiha explained that her husband knew nothing about the matter because he didn't have the money; she had borrowed it from her brother in order to come there. And so the sheikha felt sorry for Nabiha's plight and permitted her to pee on the amulet instead of her husband, on condition that she made a point of saying, "I hereby urinate on behalf of my husband so-and-so, son of so-and-so (name of mother)."

When the two women returned from their long and exhausting travels, for some reason Aisha had the feeling that they had switched amulets. The one Nabiha had was hers, and vice versa. Nabiha's heart became filled with fear, so she exchanged amulets with Aisha. They proceeded to carry out the sheikha's instructions, feeling doubtful about the exchange they had made.

Nabiha told me the story of the "trip to the Beqaa" and how Aisha had been certain, during her pregnancy with me, that she was carrying a boy. I understood why Aisha hadn't believed it when she gave birth to a daughter rather than a son. The women asked her, "Has Jamal arrived? Has Jamal arrived?" She was going to name him Jamal after the Egyptian leader who had died during her pregnancy, whose picture was hanging in her husband's store and her father-in-law's store before that.

Speaking of Abd el-Nasser, another man comes to mind who inhabited every house in the neighborhood and possibly the entire village: Abd el-Halim.

He might have been the only person to dwell in the hearts of successive generations. Every generation embarked on adolescence, arm in arm, with Abd el-Halim and his songs. It was difficult for any competitors who entered the scene to be accepted into the ranks with Abd el-Halim. Salam's father smashed all the Midhat Saleh cassettes because, in his opinion, only Abd el-Halim was worth the money his daughter spent on those cassettes. But the older generation was defeated when Amr Diab, and others like him, stormed into their children's lives. That young man, who jumped around like a monkey on a stage, was a raging hurricane which could not be warded off. The dads had gotten old in their turn, so they withdrew from the battle and made way for "*Lawlaaki*—If Not for You" and "*Mayyaal Mayyaal*—Leaning Towards You".

The world of males was like a subterranean vault. The story didn't end at the coffee house but evolved successively in that most abundant beehive of theirs known as the School for Boys, and our school was the School for Girls.

When the teachers became aware the boys had been heading directly to the entrance of the girls' school, or its vicinity, to watch them on their way out, they tried to control the situation by delaying the boys' dismissal fifteen minutes after the girls' dismissal time.

But that didn't help. The girls dawdled and the boys skipped out early.

I used to see the older schoolgirls crouching in corners and dark places-stairways or a vacant house-, chatting with boys or men who slipped things into their hands and pockets—letters and gifts of cassette tapes. They met during breaks when it wasn't as crowded as at the end of the school day or during "dismissal". During these opportune moments, Hammoudeh lay in wait for Jihan to woo her, and the baker's son gave my sister Saada a Hany Shaker tape, which she didn't stop playing for days, to the point that she was singing it in her sleep: *Asaahib meen? W ya raytik maaaya…* 'Who shall I befriend? How I wish you were with me…' And my sister Saadiyya's school uniform got torn. She wasn't wearing a blouse underneath it, so part of her stomach and belly button were exposed in front of Jamal, the butcher's son. He started waiting for her every day at the same time. Then he joined the army to make himself eligible to ask for her hand in marriage, the big event that came to be known in Aisha's household as "the first wedding."

"Dismissal" was a real festival—commotion and yelling and noise. Lots of people and cars and peddlers selling things—pretzels, cotton candy, salted nuts and make-up kits…with young men taking the opportunity to catch a wink, a glance or a letter if possible. They would climb up onto the wall that surrounded the school, so they could watch the girls.

In their turn, the girls became flustered by the mere awareness of the presence of the opposite sex watching them. That was why they pulled out the eyeliner and the lipstick before exiting the school. And many of them would hike up their skirts, shortening them a bit, while others took off their uniform aprons, so their thighs, which were stuffed inside tight jeans, could take in the boys' hot breaths that saturated the air around the school.

I didn't look down on their behavior, but I didn't understand it, either. Why should they go to any special trouble for a man's sake?

Hadn't they seen what roosters do? How they go from one hen to another all day long and then turn their backs on the young chicks as if they have no connection to them at all.

Hadn't they seen the tomcats? Especially in the winter, during mating season? How they fight until they draw blood, and some of them pluck out the eyes of other tomcats just to mate with a female. They start making roaring sounds that hearken back to their ferocious, killer origins, forgetting a long history of domestication and taming by humans. After mating, the matter transcends the worst criminal imagination when the tomcats kill their young so they can mate again with the bereaved mother.

My grandmother used to rescue the newborn kittens and move them from one place to another during late winter and early spring.

Once, Umm Najib said to her, disapprovingly, "Let him eat them. If not for that, we'd have cats coming out our ears."

I never divulged to anyone the happiness which used to flood over me whenever my grandmother was choosing a rooster to butcher, relieving the hens of him. We never ever butchered a hen. We never forsook a single one until she'd run out of years. The ensuing grief was too great to describe. Her voice trembling, my grandmother would tell me, "The gray hen has died," and sorrow would paralyze my limbs.

I tried once to revive a dying hen. I gave her drops of *mazaher* to drink like we do to revive people when they pass out. But I didn't succeed. That hen did not display the least desire to live.

In difficult circumstances, I most often turned to *mazaher*, my dearest and most successful amulet.

A few days after my grandmother died, as I was leaving the house to go to the co-op, I slammed the door shut as usual and then felt something rain down behind me.

I turned to look and saw the bitter orange blossoms spread all over the ground, around the tree trunk. I didn't think that slamming the door had been the cause. Rather, the flowers must have fallen over the course of a few days without my noticing and wanted to remind me that morning it was time to distill the *mazaher*.

I almost continued on my way, but then I said to myself, "While my grandmother was alive, she would never leave the flowers to wilt beneath their mother!" It wasn't right to let their beautiful fragrance vanish into thin air.

That is why I put down my purse and knelt beneath the tree to gather the flowers into a pillowcase which had been hanging on the clothesline.

I apologized to the flowers in silence, with fingers trembling in repentance.

Mazaher is the flower's soul. We pick the flower, pluck its petals and soak it in hot water. Then we bring it to the boil, and it cries in pain. Its tears store away the juices of its soul.

I am thinking about something as I guard the *karkeh* distiller from the squabbling cats: the beautiful *narenj*—bitter orange—blossoms are boiling over the open flame...perhaps it is from here that it gets its name, "*Nar—enj*". In the sea of *Nar* -fire- it appeals for help from drowning, burning and boiling, but no one pays any heed. A few drops from its steam are rescued and become concentrated perfume. I think that the origin of the word *narenj* is a blending of the two words: *nar*—fire—and *en-najaat*—salvation.

It drips, drop by drop, unhurried, in a steady rhythm. We collect the drops in glass vials and store them for a period of time before selling them.

Mazaher consoles us during crowded funerals. We sprinkle the soul of the bitter orange onto the grief-stricken and those who have fainted. It heals people ailing from mental illness and depression and despair… And it livens up desserts, too, and soothes colic and nursing mothers.

It's no small matter for the soul of a fragrant flower like the bitter orange blossom to do such a thing.

I put a few drops of *mazaher* into the batter for the *Aish al-Saraya* dessert. I have soaked the dry toast in honey and, on top of it, I will add a layer of cream I will make from milk, starch, *maward*—rose water—and *mazaher*. The final touch will be to garnish the dish with a generous sprinkling of ground pistachios, almond slices and some coconut. But I am going to improvise today and put a layer of sliced fruit in the middle.

Is such improvising appropriate?

I hesitate. I've never been this way in the kitchen. People have cured their ailments with music, medicines, herbs, and even illusions, but I cured myself with cooking.

Only in the kitchen could I regain my self-confidence and become an expert. Even when I'm writing to you, I don't feel the happiness I feel when I am cooking. The contrast is clear—what I write, ends up in the waste basket whereas what I cook, ends up in the brain.

The flavors of those foods stay on the palate of those who taste them, and in their memories, too.

How many times did visitors seek us out just to taste my cooking! How many times did I hope that news of my fine skills would reach you when you came to the neighborhood for a visit.

The news did reach some of my former teachers although they didn't believe it. They all said I was a stupid girl who couldn't possibly be good at anything.

I know you won't believe them. In the kitchen, numbers are unimportant; arranging letters properly to form words is useless. The important thing is the meaning of the word, the picture, the taste, and the smell formed when you think of that word or when you hear it.

What is there to gain from writing the word "basil" if you don't smell its fragrance whenever you say or write the word? If you don't remember its leaves on *Eid* mornings, on the graves, the women in their white headscarves and black dresses, offering the most beautiful and powerful plants to the bones of their lost loved ones beneath the ground?

What is the difference between writing the word "yeast" if you don't know the way brown bubbles appear when you mix the yeast with flour and water? How it resides in the dough and starts growing bigger and wider, only beginning to swell in longing for the coming fire? How it makes the scanty, dry lump of dough into a blessed ball, swollen with promises of satiating hunger and giving the most delicious pleasure?

What do you need kilos and grams for when you have the palm of your hand to measure with?

I have no need for lessons in arithmetic or science or even culture or history here in this small, secluded place away from people. Here, I am not ashamed of my ugliness since no one sees me, but a beautiful picture will be drawn on the dish into which I will ladle what I've cooked.

I imagine I am there, where there are no mirrors or glass windows—beautiful like the ghoul's daughter, Sitt Budour, the beautiful *houri* and Sitt al-Husn. They are all me, and you approach like a ghost from behind my back to look over my shoulder at what I'm making in the kitchen. And you ask me questions, such as:

Why did I put the block of cheese in the freezer before grating it? To make it easier to grate it. The fats in it solidify, so it hardens.

Why am I adding so many chopped tomatoes to the salad? And so I tell you I am making spicy potatoes and, since potatoes sometimes get stuck in the throat, tomatoes are a good way to ease swallowing in that case.

And you ask me why I don't chop the mint along with the parsley, so I tell you that mint is very tender and reacts quickly to the air. That's why it turns black when we chop it with a knife. So, I leave it until the final touch, helping it to stay green in the dish.

And you ask me about love, so I tell you that love is to cook with all your senses and all your imagination—not with your brain, weighing scales and measuring cups. How many a woman has carefully followed recipes from cookbooks, yet did not succeed in bringing happiness to her loved ones? Most likely, she lost them because she failed to consider her heart and listened instead to a stupid cookbook.

I hate people who think cooking is a silly endeavor and don't see what an art it is. They don't know its secrets are not simple and that the very mixing of ingredients sometimes makes poetry, sometimes epics, and sometimes it makes very bad literature.

When I talk to the workers at the co-op about cooking, some of them grumble and consider women to be silly people who have nothing to talk about besides cooking. Only those who cook to satisfy hunger are like that. As for someone who cooks in order to heal, in order to bring joy, in order to release sorrows, in order to love, and in order to wipe away some injustice, that person doesn't just cook, but resurrects an alternate life in order to keep standing on two feet, in spite of the abusive words assailing her.

Whoever said we either eat to live, or live to eat?! What a superficial, pretentious, and crude idealism! Why can't we do both things at the same time? Eat and live. Why do they see food as something lower than life when it is one of life's sources of support, like love or motherhood? Or friendship or art or medicine or science or music?

***

"This world is a book…and you are the thoughts within it / This world is a series of nights…and you are the life that is lived / This world is eyes…and you are vision / This world is a sky…and you are the moon / This is how I bear living my life…in blessing and torture…"

Umm Kulthum burns with emotion in the cassette which is as old as I am. She sang that song in '71, and

I was born at the end of 1970. In a few months, I will be thirty, but, if I live that long, I will enter my thirties holding the soft touch of your handshake with the imprint of your face in my vision and my heart.

Umm Kulthum burns. Her heart catches fire and so does the street outside. The high temperature turns it into a forsaken place, like a desert where vipers make their nests in the sand, and its midday heat causes the trees to wither as they bend over in pain.

Umm Kulthum's voice vanishes at the usual place and the usual time. I know the reason well. The tape got torn previously, so I removed the screws and took it apart. Then I fused the tape together with nail polish, which is a trick only the cassette tape generation knows.

But 'Souma' didn't finish the song. I go to check the tape player and the cassette to find the tape has broken right at the spot where the remnants of nail polish were. I know exactly what this is—a bad sign.

For a decade and a half, I've been listening to that tape. All that time since I mended it, and it hasn't broken until today.

My heart is telling me you will not come.

I think about something I hadn't considered. A lot of people fail to show up at invitations and meetings, especially with people they don't know. What is going to encourage you to come, in spite of the heat, and the fact that you're busy and traveling early tomorrow morning?

I made a big mistake not giving you compelling reasons to come. I didn't tell you who I am.

But I don't want to tell you. That will make me lose my nerve.

I wish I had given you some sort of sign—a puzzle to solve or some incentive, but what can I do now? Mere hours before the appointment time upon which my life is suspended?

How? What can I say to make you come?

Plan A: I am sick, and you are the only doctor I know here since I moved only recently to Beirut. I'm all alone. No relatives or friends. Please help me.

You might say, "Call an ambulance."

Plan B: I am from the same village as you, one of the closest people to you, and there's an urgent matter I want to discuss with you.

But I'm reminded of what your friend Hassan said after your famous falling-out—you hate everything which brings you back to the past. He spread that everywhere to mar your image and, it seems to me, to take revenge on you for your success. Any talk about the past is not going to make you happy. It will put an end to any hope of your coming.

Plan C: I tell you the plain and simple truth. I have loved you since childhood, and I live for the chance to be together no matter how impossible it might be. Will you make the impossible possible and come, even for half an hour?

You will think I am crazy, and you will discover that I lied when I called the first time, pretending to be a researcher doing a study on the life of Lebanese in Russia. A bad plan. Like the other two before it.

The fish almost burns. I rescue half of it, but the other half is badly over fried. It has lost its moistness and its ability to adorn the dish of *Siyyadiyeh*.

Now begins the clumsiness and bad luck I had been expecting all along. I'm considering burning myself and screaming for help.

I peel the onions and, right on cue, comes a bout of crying just when I need it to defuse my anxiety and bewilderment and maybe even turn my luck around. "It's going to be okay," I repeat like a parrot, hoping to make myself believe my own words.

I drop the onions into the same hot oil I fried the fish in. That is the most important secret to *Siyyadieh* which, if ignored by the cook, will surely end in total failure.

Despite my precautions, the smell of fish creeps into the apartment. What can I do now? The first thing which comes to mind is to make a dessert with a lot of vanilla. The most wonderful houses are those with the scent of vanilla emanating from them.

I've never forgotten the house of Umm Badeea—mother of seven sons—as was her claim to fame in the village. She used to keep the shoe bin right at the entrance to the house. Whenever she opened the front door for me, I would be assailed by the odor of her sons' shoes! Rubber, oil, sandals and the sweat of all those boys' feet.

I used to hate it when my grandmother sent me to deliver something to Umm Badeea. I would hold my breath as I traversed the long hallway between the front door and the kitchen. It was a very long distance despite being no more than five steps—five steps replete with the smell of the shoes of those males I didn't like even when they were squeaky clean!

But one day, as I headed towards the kitchen with the dandelion leaves my grandmother had harvested for Umm Badeea, I felt the urge to stop.

The shoe bin was out getting some sun on the porch, and Umm Badeea was cooking something which smelled just like my dreams on summer nights.

I forgave Umm Badeea and her seven sons for every moment of discomfort I'd lived through inside their house.

I continued to call it "vanillia" as Umm Badeea had pronounced it at the time, until I started working at the co-op and discovered it was pronounced "vanilla".

O delicate vanilla, come to my aid.

What shall I tell him to make him come? Shall I send him a text message? Something like: I have a secret you will want to know. Don't forget about our appointment.

Or: I'm begging you! Many of my other research participants have had to cancel. You're my last hope. Don't skip our appointment. My professional life is in your hands.

Overdone. Not realistic.

Or: I'm all alone and feeling sad tonight.

Or…or… I continue asking myself as I remove the fish bones.

***

Tired out from all the thinking, I turn on the television for a short break.

I don't like the cooking shows on television. They present the recipes like a commodity and promote the chefs. Some of them turn into superstars who put on big festivals and book signing parties for books which don't contain a single bit of information about the truth of cooking—what it conceals within itself in terms of stories of love and hate and passion and deprivation…

They don't know, for example, why folks in rural areas depended on bulgur wheat, but I do.

If I were directing one of those shows, I would tell the story of a peasant who toils all day long and drips with sweat, who requires effective nourishment to build up his body like the foundation of a house—with cement. Bulghur was the body's cement. That is my word for it. As for the peasants, they called it by another name: Nails for the Knees. And when rice became prevalent in our country, coming from faraway lands, it was said, "Rice came into its heyday and bulghur put a noose around its neck."

The proof of bulghur's death sentence is tabbouleh. Bulghur used to be the main ingredient of that dish—a lot of bulghur garnished with some tomatoes, parsley and green onions. Nowadays, little remains of that large amount but a mere spattering—a light sprinkle of bulghur over the most famous salad given to visiting tourists. Originally, it was never a salad, nor did it have the least bit to do with tourists.

Aisha's two knees that nearly choked me to death one day are the legacy of this bulghur mania.

I don't remember when Aisha got so heavy. Did she get fat all of a sudden? Or am I the one who didn't notice? Who ignored everything that had to do with her? Her height, her obesity, and her sitting around at the store were matters that, in my mind, made her the perfect image of the giant of scary fairytales.

I saw her a while after that battle of ours. She was sitting, bent down over her stomach and torso. Her shoulders were huge and hefty, and when she tried to stand up, she was unable to straighten her spinal column as needed. She looked just like her maternal uncle with her hands dangling below her waist.

When I used to catch sight of her—by coincidence—I would ask myself how she was able to function with that body of hers. How did she manage to sponge herself when bathing? How did the seamstress take her measurements? How did she get into a taxi when she went to Sidon? Where did she take that colossal body of hers at night when she lay down on her bed? And did my sisters think about that before they got married? Did they think it was a good idea to get married as soon as possible, so their nights would become more welcoming?

All of that came to an end when illness melted away her fat and her flesh.

I hoped sleeping would become easier, more merciful, but I lived through worse nightmares while awake than the ones I saw in my dreams. This is why I don't differentiate between reality and dreams and don't care to differentiate or separate them. The truth is I am not interested in living one long succession of wakefulness or one long dream… It's all the same.

The pain is the same. What hurts me in either state has the same effect—leaves the same scars and the same memories.

Sometimes, when a nightmare wakes me up, I don't find myself in bed but in a big hall with velvet upholstered seats, surrounded by curtains that emanate sweet-smelling fragrances. And I hear the sounds of bodies leaving and clothing rubbing against thighs, legs and arms. I don't turn to look. I wait for everything to quieten down.

Everyone leaves, but I continue to wait for some unknown thing.

For this to be true. Not a daydream.

***

The cell phone rings.

"Hello."

"Hello…Yes, Hello."

"Hel…"

"Hello?… Can you hear me? Miss Tayma Safadiyya?"

I almost said no. I had completely forgotten the name I'd invented for myself.

I had chosen a Sidon family name because I learned the Sidon accent from working at the lunchmeat factory.

"Ye…Yes…"

"How are you?"

"F…Fine…"

"Good, I'm…"

I thought you were going to apologize and say you couldn't come.

"Sorry, but concerning the interview today… I wanted…"

The line gets disconnected, or maybe in my flustered state I hung up by mistake. Sadness presses on my heart, pain in my chest. Millions of flowers boil in the lava of a volcano.

I don't know how to reach you. The numbers and buttons on this stupid device bewilder me.

The phone rings again.

"I got cut off… It's a weak signal…but quickly… about today…What time is the appointment exactly? I forgot. Seven or six?"

I smile.

"Six…uhhh…no seven…seven…seven."

"Umm…Actually I can't make it at seven…Could we make it six? I have some work I have to do at 7:30 and tomorrow morning I'm going back to Moscow."

"… Six. Do… do you need the address?"

"Yes, that would be wonderful. You read my mind."

I did indeed read your mind, but that's ancient history. What is in your mind now, I wonder.

But wait! How could I have agreed to an earlier time? I won't be ready at six. According to my detailed itinerary, I won't be ready!

I've lost an hour from my calculations. Now, I'll have to compensate somehow.

***

The policeman said, "Go left."

I thanked him and went on my way. I didn't let on that it would take me a little while to determine left from right.

I stopped at the corner trying to figure out which way was left, so I could get to the damned coiffeur.

In the ad, I had seen the way he transformed ugly women into beauties. Before and After. An expensive magician, but I didn't care how much I had to pay him to have the encounter of a lifetime. My biggest dream is for you to see me beautiful, despite all my doubts you can possibly find beauty in a soul that doesn't believe it possesses any.

This is the hand I hold a knife with—must be the right. I curl my fingers into a fist as though I'm grabbing hold of a knife and cut the air with it. Yes, that's the one. So, the other empty hand with outstretched fingers must be the left. I should go that way.

***

"Your hair's strong, not coarse…Don't worry. It's

going to come out great...Let's style it curly. What do you think?"

The idea did not appeal to me. I want straight hair, but the hairdresser reminded me of something when he added, "It'll be just like a *houri's* hair." Then he uttered "*bismillah*" after seeing such long and luxurious hair. Was this magician really going to turn me into a *houri*, just as I had always dreamed? Just as the fairy godmother did to Cinderella?

Do you like wavy hair? Are you enticed by the slender waists of the *houris* and their bottoms? Will the dress I chose, which is tight at the waist and buttocks, revive memories of your grandmother's fairytales? Or don't you remember that past you fled from willfully and with full awareness, leaving behind more than one broken heart?

How will I make you understand that wounds get handed down, and the pus that oozes from them becomes an antidote for other wounds?

I recline in the long chair at the beauty parlor.

I feel cold. As Yvonne explained, the air conditioning is on full blast to ensure success with the makeup. This means I will arrive home looking like a ghoul after all the different colors of makeup melt and my curly hair puffs up into a mess!

I close my eyes, so I can dream of leaving there as a

beautiful woman. Another woman. But whoever said you are enamored with beautiful women? Didn't you leave that beautiful fiancée of yours? Didn't you marry a Russian woman of only mediocre beauty? Your buddies all made fun of your taste when you brought her to the village for a visit that time.

Who is that woman looking at me?

After a few seconds, I discover I am in front of a giant mirror, and the woman in the mirror is me.

Yvonne said it wasn't magic, but rather the bringing out of details that had been hidden. And the hairdresser said cutting long hair into layers gives it that rich and beautiful shape, sets it free. He brushes off a few wisps, pleased with his creation.

***

I get into the first taxi to stop for me.

All I can think about are the few hours separating me from your arrival time. I am not going to think about the possibility you're not coming because that thought makes me feel paralyzed.

The streets zip by behind the window of the air-conditioned car as it pants and moans from the heaviness and slowness of the heat. Alone inside my chest, that heart of mine runs, racing past the minutes and getting to the moment of your arrival. A comforting song is coming from the taxi radio. I don't understand a word of it, or maybe I don't remember the words from being under so much stress.

***

The taxi drops me off.

It takes me three minutes to realize that I'm on the wrong street. It resembles the street where I took up residence two days ago, but it's not it. It might be across from it or an extension of it, but it's not the street.

I turn and circle around the buildings, the shops and the many cars.

There is a man pushing a cart of wilted vegetables. I feel like one of his vegetables. I ask him where Armenia Street is, but he ignores me, not because he doesn't know but perhaps because he doesn't feel like talking.

He goes on his way. A leaf of lettuce falls from his cart. The edges are dry and withered. When it hits the ground, it sounds like the thud of a corpse being tossed from a speeding car.

I look at the time.

6:01.

Right now, you're at the door to the apartment ringing the doorbell and no one is answering.

No one opens the door because I am stuck on some

street somewhere, and I don't know how to get to where my apartment is supposed to be.

How did I think of everything except this?

I start trembling, nervous and angry at myself for my stupidity. I try to get a hold of myself and concentrate. I retrace how I'd left the house. Figuring which way I went when I left will guide me how to get back.

I left the apartment and, at the entrance of my building, I hailed a taxi. He took me to the corner and then to another street, then another, then…no…I don't remember.

I look up at the sky, appealing for help.

Then I decide just to walk in any direction. Maybe I will find the yellow building that's across the street from my building because I can't remember the color of my own building or what it looks like.

And the reason is simple. I was inside the building and couldn't see it. It never occurred to me when entering or exiting to look—to lift my head up and look at it. The only thing I was looking at was where my feet were stepping, so I wouldn't trip.

I turn all the way around. In spite of me, a teardrop falls from my eye.

I come back to find the lettuce leaf. It is totally brown. The heat has been preventing me from thinking—the same way it prevents people from walking around outside. I see a friendly face coming towards me—an elegant figure so familiar it's as though I'd been running into him on this same street for years.

As he comes forward, his smile widens. I sense he is preparing to extend his hand towards me and wave his arm to signal to me, but he walks right past without seeing me.

He leaves me dumbfounded, tasting the salty tear that has dried up above my lip.

A dash of salt—at just the right time. I needed it for balance—just like when I make desserts and add a little salt to the sugar in order to create contrast and balance at the same time.

I am stuck in my place like a stubborn rusty nail no one thinks to yank out.

But then I see a gray-streaked head looking all around as if searching for some address. I follow him until he leads me to the stray building.

I go ahead of him and request the elevator. We get on and the doors close.

My heart freezes like a piece of fruit inside a block of ice. I don't look up. I bow my head in silence. I look down at my feet, at my French manicure and his shoes.

Dear God! What kind of a mess am I in? His breaths are all in my lungs. The heat of his pulse. A strange smoky smell unlike any smoke I've ever smelled.

No trace of his first cologne.

What shall I do?

He is here. A mere footstep separates us. He is closer than I ever dreamed he would be. Do I hug him? Do I hit him? Or fall down so he'll catch me?

But I do what he was not expecting me to do. I start humming in my heart what I had just heard in the taxi, to distract myself from its confusion and embarrassment and anxiety.

"There is no past that I can say ever was…One that you have neither remembered nor forgotten. We've never been brought together in one place, so that you would know what I have suffered…Oh how I wish your heart would remember me, even if you hate me and I love you…"

Only here, do I grasp the meaning of the words… because it is the song that went astray.

It is my song for you. I discovered both of you together right here in a cramped elevator running out of oxygen and mercy.

With difficulty, I brace myself to prevent fainting.

Fifth floor.

The door to the apartment from which the smells of *Siyyadieh* and vanilla emanate in a discordant duet.

Part Three

A solitary patch of sky looks down upon the woman with the curly hair, but not for very long. A mean cloud stretches across the sky and hides her face on the verge of tears.

The light breezes which had been toying with the curtains of the building across the street have turned into wind gusts. She understands that the cloud hadn't been targeting her but rather the entire city.

That split second took away her desire to watch Tim as he walked away down the street. Maybe because it hadn't been an urgent and true desire. She let him go in peace, thanking him for the air he set into motion on his way out. Grateful for the emptiness he left behind.

She closed her eyes for a few seconds and, when she opened them, he wasn't in the street.

She feels a drop of water. A second drop, and a third…

She can't believe it is rain—as if she too had never seen it before or knew it existed!

She sticks her hand out of the window and catches the large drops that splash on her sad pores.

She sees people going out into the street, and hands of all sizes and colors coming out of windows… Adults, children and elderly folks peering out from balconies. Except the stripper.

She rushes to the closet and, without thinking, takes out the mulberry dress and puts it on. She has an overwhelming desire to celebrate.

She puts on the white sandals…and then goes outside.

She walks with heavy steps, paying no attention to anyone but, despite the rain drenching her, after a few steps, she feels herself getting lighter and lighter… So she resolves to keep walking and get lost all over again since nothing is waiting for her, and she isn't waiting for anyone.

A few of Tim's sentences follow her, so she speeds up her steps trying to flee from them.

She wants so badly to believe that he didn't come.

***

Her hand started bleeding again—bright red, cooled by the rain.

As she walks, she removes the bandage and inspects the wound. She remembers when the love of her life shut the door—without meaning to—on her hand and she let out that muffled cry. Frightened, he came back and stammered that he was about to leave.

She reached out ahead of him with her good hand and said she was fine while simultaneously trying to retrieve her soul from deep inside her.

Did he really mean to leave? Or was it just a moment of confusion and fear? Was he worried about her or about himself? Or did he feel guilty towards her?

The rain dies down, so she sits on a bench at the entrance to one of the university buildings.

She used to dream of going to the university. But—speaking of dreams—why should she be sad when her biggest dream had come true with today's encounter?

The wound on her hand was clear proof he had come.

The dirt smells musty, heavy with dust. It resembles the taste of the bite of food she was swallowing when he mentioned there was a racetrack not far from her building, and many people from his village had gotten addicted to those games. One of them was even called "*Sahbeh*"—"Lottery" which was a light form of gambling. That man had committed suicide.

Committed suicide? Did he say that her father committed suicide? She didn't dare ask him. Her veins turned blue.

How could she not have known all those years? Had no one ever mentioned it in front of her? Had no one's tongue slipped? Out of the hundreds of chatterboxes surrounding her?

Does the manner of death change the way we feel about the one who is killed? Whether death killed him, or he killed himself… What difference does it make?

Sadness overcomes her as water drips from the ends of her long hair onto that strange bench. She weeps for her father as if his blood were still warm beneath the ground. She sobs for the exasperation she swallowed an hour ago and couldn't express.

Her flushed face had turned into a burning ember. When she rushed to the kitchen and opened the freezer to cool it, her fingers in contrast were like the chunks of ice inside the freezer.

She couldn't see where the dessert was, but she wasn't really searching for the plates and the fruit. Instead, she saw the brook and the valley and herself plummeting, weightless, in a flowing linen dress while her bird flew off towards the sea.

She looked at the dessert in despair. She had made it with such care and uneasiness—the same condition she had been in for everything she made.

She almost asked him, "What did you do with my letter?" But she delayed asking, expecting him to bring up the letter by chance. That was the way he had mentioned other matters as part of the research chatter she had prepared for him and during which he went off on tangents talking about his personal memories.

The letter? Yes, that letter. He hadn't forgotten it even though he didn't keep it for more than a few minutes.

There were things that seemed to be dear to the heart of whoever had written it. It had been written with a great deal of sincerity, so it was difficult to know how to deal with it.

He couldn't keep it. He disposed of it just as he had disposed of his girlfriends.

It wasn't just a letter he was trying to get rid of, but rather a bit of real evidence that might enrage his wife.

His wife possessed a sixth sense about things related to his heart. She would know when he was on the verge of a fleeting relationship, or in the vast sea of a deep relationship—a false love or a true one. She could even guess the places he might invite his girlfriends to. That was why he never kept anything connected to another woman.

He got rid of everything, even memories. But he didn't dare tear up, burn or keep that letter.

He put it on the seat beside him in the car and took off without a plan. He drove his car through the streets like someone transporting the dead body of a person he had just strangled, with the national security hot on his trail.

He settled on leaving it amidst some green grass in a forest.

He knew that the garbage collectors wouldn't see it, and no meddlers would find it. The snow and the rain would fall on it, and it would disintegrate on its own without pain or insult.

Before he left, a summer rain fell not unexpectedly and gave rise to a shocking scent of orange blossoms. He looked all around himself searching for the source, for a bitter orange tree somewhere in his surroundings.

He touched the ink that had started to run down the envelope and sniffed it. It smelled of *mazaher*, an aroma he had nearly forgotten.

Images of numerous women hovered in his memory, one of which was Fatima, but his knowledge of her writing abilities edged her outside the realm of possibility. Beautiful Fatima hadn't made any mistake except that, with her innate ignorance, she would have tied him up like a bull in his little village brook. He would never be able to achieve the dream he'd always dreamed of and vigilantly kept to himself: the cinema.

He had come back that day soaking wet to his little office at the television station.

Excited and boisterous, he started writing what would be the script for his first documentary film. His writing was only semi-readable because his ideas got ahead of his fingers, and he wanted to catch them before they could slip away as had happened to him over the years.

Anyone who knew Arabic well could discern in those pages which reeked of the sweat of his hands and traces of the *mazaher* and the moist forest grass, that the film, whose idea he had waited so long for heaven to inspire him with, was about the bitter orange tree.

He wrote while bringing back to his mind every detail about that tree. He discovered a lot of information had been hiding in his memory, and all he had needed to bring it to the surface was that letter.

That scent had always been there, in his hidden room in the garden. It used to emanate from between his books and papers; it was lodged in the velvet of his chair. It didn't come from the garden as he had assumed haphazardly, not having had cause to think about it or analyze it. But now he was analyzing: he used to visit that room in the summer, and there aren't any orange blossoms in summer, so then how did the fragrance get into his locked room?

From his pockets and desk drawers, he removed all the scraps of paper which he had promised to let see daylight someday.

That day had finally come.

He found a lot in them about the tree that had struggled so hard to live and to last until today. Even when they punished it with the heat and drought of deserts, it lived.

All the experts say it first appeared in China; it is mentioned in the earliest Chinese books.

But his heart rejected that historical supposition.

He read the situation as follows: The tree hadn't first appeared in China, but paper had first been known in China and, consequently, writing on paper, which could be circulated easily. It is possible for whoever possesses precedence in writing something down to attribute to himself all manner of victories and valuable things.

A tree with such endurance, stubbornness, and vitality would undoubtedly spread to numerous locations on earth. The strong fragrance of its blossoms attracted lots of insects which, while believing they'd been born for the sole purpose of sucking the nectar of flowers, were actually taking upon themselves the most important of roles in the history of creation: pollination of the plant kingdom. How could they have believed flowers could be so naïve as to guide the insects to their delicious nectar with that powerful fragrance for nothing in return? The bitter orange trees didn't care about the insects' hunger; they wanted to be victorious in the battle for survival.

On one of the slips of paper, he found scattered words more like a puzzle:

Renj = pain

Na = unknown

Na + renj = unknown pain

Nar + renj = an unfinished group

He now realized on that day in the distant past, he had written down what the words meant in Persian and Chinese and Turkish…But those words didn't mean anything.

He wrote the film *Tears of the Bitter Orange Tree*. He produced it and screened it.

It was his true creation.

He opened his film with the following introduction:

According to the legend that I found amidst the thorns of the cactus pear and the terebinth tree, the orange had long been born bitter until a goddess fell in love with its colors and its fragrance. And so, she made it sweet, so she could eat its fruit. But some oranges rebelled or were defiant towards love and, until today, would not relinquish their bitterness.

The film was enchanting to the degree that it made many foreigners believe there really was an eastern legend like that.

While he was watching the birth of the tree and the transformation of its flowers into fragrant tears, the chambers of his heart were illuminated, and he inscribed his own history. He was that plant that had searched for a suitable empty space, for enough silence to hear every letter of his subdued, whispered ideas. It didn't matter if it was a hermitage amidst the snow or amidst the desert. It was merely a difference in color. The prison was one and the same.

After *Tears of the Bitter Orange Tree*, he directed several short documentaries as part of a Russian television project exploring the Arab world. He moved between various Arab cities, and Beirut was always on the list, for work or transit.

He was supposed to produce a film about Umm Kulthum. While doing research on her songs, he discovered the secret behind the song, "*A ghadan alqaak*—Will I meet you tomorrow" was not just as he and many others like him had expected. The simple story was that "*al-Sitt*" Umm Kulthum had agreed to Abdel Wahab's strategy to sing lyrics by poets from a variety of Arab nationalities and, when he was looking for something by a Sudanese poet, he came across a poem he liked by Elhadi Adam called "*A ghadan alqaak.*"

She hadn't sung it, then, for a man she was waiting for. This was about to sadden the woman who learned that fact around a dinner table from where steaming dishes arose with the most appetizing and seductive aromas. It wasn't until the director, who was chewing a mouthful of fava beans seasoned with a light touch of fresh coriander said, "She didn't sing it for a man she was waiting for, but for every woman waiting for a man."

He told her the game of waiting had always allured him. But then when he started traveling a lot and spending hours of his lifetime waiting for planes and trains, waiting became gut wrenchingly painful. Something resembling hunger, he told her. He didn't understand why her eyes lit up.

She had guessed that in those hours of waiting, he would contemplate, remember and imagine.

Undoubtedly, he would have remembered her letter, the dried flowers and the fragrances she left in his room, and they would make him hungry for an unknown love which at this point had become more like two nearly extinguished eyes.

That was why her eyes lit up—because the pain in his gut might well be the pain of love.

He wasn't aware of it, but he really was searching for an unknown love—like a blind man putting his hands out in front of himself, his chin in the air, despite knowing he's walking under the open sky.

He wanted the hero of his first dramatic film to be a blind man, but something important had ruined the project. He tried to live as a blind man for a few days, but he failed miserably.

***

He didn't intend to interrogate her, but he became suspicious when he saw food in a place that was supposed to be for work and research.

She presented all sorts of excuses and was even more flustered than she had anticipated. She was so flustered, it caused her to say a word which rescued her from making even more blunders—a word that led him to interrupt her.

He motioned with his hand for her to "slow down." He closed his eyes and started repeating the word as if he would take off and fly with it.

He hadn't heard that word in years: "*Amsaani.*"

She'd never thought about the essence of that word before, but he had taken it apart so he could piece it back together carefully: *Ams al-thaani*—the second yesterday. A little bit further back than *Ams al-awwal*—the first yesterday—the day before yesterday. The yesterday a little further back from this past day. And the yesterday a little closer to this present day.

Over many years, he had searched for that lost word to use in a line in a scenario he was writing, and which he kept chasing after like a ghost. This was so even after the draft for the scenario had become merely a dream with no hope of ever being realized.

"*Amsaani,*" he said with a smile. And that was his first real smile since he'd entered the apartment.

And that was the second smile of his she'd seen face to face, the difference between the two being the first was closer and fresher, with no wrinkles, and more than two decades of time had passed. In other words, most of her life.

***

She was disappointed. *Moghrabieh* was not his favorite dish; it was *Maqloubeh*—'upside down' dish.

He didn't say so openly, but as he was talking about his only dramatic film project, he said he imitated a smart method which women follow to make a most amazing dish: placing the expensive and appetizing ingredients at the bottom of the pot, so they will be the first to be freed from their chains when the pot is flipped over. "Genius. Genius," he repeated.

And in her heart, she repeated: Stupid…Stupid! How could she have forgotten *Maqloubeh*? Why wasn't it on her menu?

He too walks in the rain, and another raindrop falls on his head as he recalls his encounter with that strange young woman. It's a heavy rain—so heavy, tender herbs sprout in his memory.

He recalls the scene when he shut the door on her hand, and he wonders: Doesn't he know that agonized look? Hadn't he treated her once? Hadn't he smelled the scent of her skin mixed with *mazaher*? Yes, he had. But he couldn't remember where and when. He had been embarrassed by his mistake. He had rushed to come to her aid as he apologized and said he was leaving.

When she had held back from crying, her hair got tucked behind her ear, and he saw a raised scar. It was like a bottom lip preparing to receive its first kiss. He knew that scar, too. Yes, he knew her.

***

A few light drops of drizzle sprinkle down from high clouds, like the silent tears she'd shed as she was dumping the *Aish al-Saraya* dessert into the garbage and recalling how he had refused it, "No thank you… I don't like sweets."

The whole matter had headed in the wrong direction.

Just like love, there is always something missing. Just like planning for tomorrow, there is a lot of room for error. Just like making perfumes, there is a small amount of impurity. Likewise, with cooking, there is a little flaw with the measurements, in the cooking time, or from going too quickly…

The thing she hadn't taken into consideration was that the man she'd prepared this lavish banquet for might already have had his fill.

When he sat with indifference before the food, it appeared there was no meaning to anything—that the flavors themselves had lost their memory and their history.

In the garden at the college, the sound of the rusty swing comes back to her.

She fears the fantasies have started overcoming her even in the middle of the day.

The cold might be to blame. Whenever she feels cold, she hears that sound.

Completely drenched, she thinks about going back to the apartment. The smell of her invited guest would have dissipated by now, and any echo of his words would have vanished.

She goes within a few steps of the open gate and finds herself standing before the entrance to a fancy building. It was from there that the swinging sound was coming. And before she crosses through entrance, she sees a young girl rocking back and forth on a swing hanging from a tree. The girl sticks out her little tongue to catch the raindrops flying off the shaken branches.

She resembles the girl in the dream but is more lively and vivid.

She goes closer to make sure the girl isn't a mirage. Before she knows what she should do or say, a woman's voice calls out. "Yara!" The swing stops and the girl leaves.

If a simple geographical error had occurred the moment her head had emerged from her mother's womb, and she had fallen onto this spot in the city, then her name would have been Yara, and she would have worn shoes and socks with satin laces, and never would have met Tim or learned of his existence. Her teachers would have known she suffered from mild dyslexia which could be diagnosed and treated—as Tim had informed her—so she could complete her education and go to the university and maybe even the school of medicine, or travel to Russia and stroll through its forests... Then, while she sat on a bench made of wood from that forest, a piece of paper would fly towards her and stick to her body. By chance it would be a love letter no one wants—not its sender and not its receiver.

***

No point in her hoping to change the past, but maybe she could fashion the days to come?

Why not have a baby, a daughter to dress up in stockings and soft dresses? She could comb her hair with tenderness and take her on an outing to an amusement park. And then, at night, tell her stories and make up happy endings to them.

Now, she understands why having children seems like such a great ambition, and the only price worth putting up with being intimate with a man.

She walks without fear of getting lost. No matter how lost she might get, she would keep going in circles around herself. That's what always happened.

A young man passes by on a motorcycle and lobs an admiring whistle at her.

She doesn't care if it was the air conditioner repair man or someone else. The important thing was the mulberry dress looked nice to whoever saw it, dry or wet.

Two hours are enough for her to retrace all her steps.

She finds the building by chance. A corner, two sidewalks, and a street are all that separate her from it.

She thinks about her invited guest getting ready to travel now, and no one calls him "*Hakim*" because he never finished his medical specialty and chose instead to work in television as a director of documentary film clips they stuff dead air time with—films that never rescued the heart of any person and never wrote a new life for anybody on the verge of demise.

But he was still there, in front of a puddle of water shaped like a tearful eye, stopping to search in the mud of his memory.

The dishes that he had immediately backed away from had the smell of his childhood and adolescence. They had been cooked with a lot of care and precision and over votive candles. Their aromas came from alleyways where a little girl with short, matted hair and terrified eyes used to play.

***

She must cross the street.

Her body trembles with that same shudder of fear which grips her when she crosses the highway to the co-op. So many times, she felt she wouldn't survive or make it to the other side.

The darkness is frightening. But she jumps with agility and grace as though she's lost half her weight.

She reaches the door of the building and, before advancing further, Tim's voice calls out…

Her name is blown to pieces in the wet sky.

"May."

The End